Proof of Death

A Laughing Loaf Bakery Mystery

Victoria Kazarian

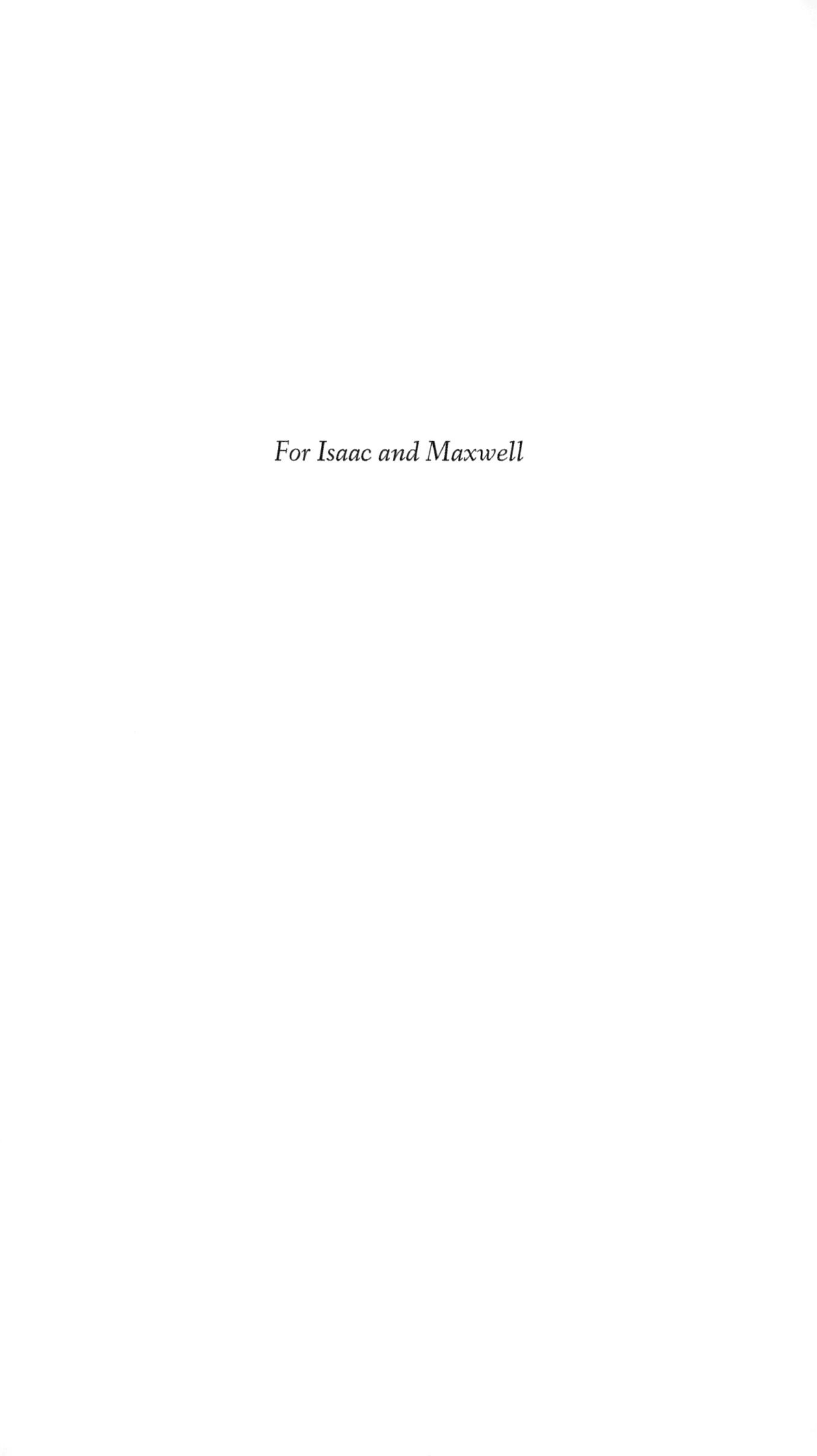

For Isaac and Maxwell

Chapter One

I f I've learned anything about working in the service industry, it's this: don't go into a business right before it closes.

I get it. Busy people put things off.

Actually, *most* people put things off.

It was 1:50 p.m. on February 13, ten minutes before closing at The Laughing Loaf Bakery.

The line at the counter snaked back to the front door—and phone calls were coming in from people eager to order last minute items for Valentine's Day.

It's not like my assistant manager Beck Rodriguez and I didn't have anything to do.

We had a back room full of holiday-themed baked goods to prepare. Beck was in full-on pastry-prep mode and was rolling out dough for the special menu we'd planned for this week. To pitch in with bread on weekdays, I'd brought on Maeve Killoran, a baker I'd met at Night Rose bakery on a trip to Sonoma with my boyfriend Nate before Christmas.

Our latest addition? We hired a teenaged delivery team, which had been making some pre-Valentines deliveries this week. They would kick into full gear tomorrow, delivering holiday treats like cherry chocolate sourdough and raspberry beignets to people in River Grove, Los Gatos, and then over to Santa Cruz and the coast.

The wrought iron hands of the big French clock on the wall of the dining area showed me it was past our closing time of 2 p.m.

But with ten people still in line, we would stay open until we'd served everyone.

River Grove Mayor Corinne Webster was first in line, which surprised me since she was a planner, the last person I'd expect to wait to the last minute.

"We're having our first meeting of the River Grove River Rats softball team on Saturday." She glanced behind her. "I know you're busy. I wanted to get my order in as soon as I thought of it."

I laughed. "Corinne, you know everyone else is here for something they want tomorrow. Or *today*. I appreciate the advanced notice. We'll have four days to get that ready for you."

"I don't want to be one of those people who waits until the last minute." The mayor cast a judgy frown on the people in line behind her.

"And I do appreciate that. Can you stop by the day after tomorrow? We can talk about what you want, and we can make something really special for the team." I smiled. Right now I had to deal with all *those* people. The mayor nodded.

"Thanks, Gracie." She made her way back past the line, still dispensing smug looks to people in line.

Okay, who was next up? This was feeling like a game of whack-a-mole.

The next face looking across the counter at me was only slightly familiar. He'd been into The Laughing Loaf a few times, but Beck had mostly dealt with him. Eddie, his name was—Eddie Sumner. He worked with Kirk at BlueSurf. From what Elana said, they did not get along.

Eddie wore a black knit beanie and a sweatshirt with the silhouette of a big, Hokusai-style wave on it—BlueSurf's logo. He pulled AirPods out of his ears. I watched him very slowly take out their case and put the earpieces away as people behind him looked on impatiently.

"I need something for my girlfriend. She got me something, so I guess that means I have to get her something, too." Eddie Sumner said glumly as he leaned over to study the display case. He tapped his fingers on the counter. "I don't want to waste any time here. What do you got?"

"We're sold out of most of today's treats, so there's not much I can give you on the spot. You can set this up for delivery to her tomorrow. How about a breakfast tray with homemade Pop Tarts? Or a loaf of cherry chocolate sourdough with a Laughing Loaf coffee mug?" I glanced again at the clock. 2:10 p.m. I was in a hurry too, especially with the rest of the prep we needed to finish to be ready for tomorrow.

He dug into his pocket and pulled out his wallet. "Fine. Laura's always talking about sourdough. Nice if I don't have to pick anything up. I mean, this is a frickin' made-up holiday anyway, right? I'm lead engineer on a very important product we're releasing at BlueSurf. I have better things to do with my time."

He slid the card into the pay station absently, while looking down at his phone.

"I hope she enjoys it." I tried to sound cheery. "It'll be delivered tomorrow between 4 and 7." I handed him an order form. "Fill out the delivery address here."

He grunted. "She'll be at my house. Her place is a

dump, and she can't stand her roommates. I'm working from home tomorrow." He scrawled the address on the form and handed it back to me. He was a block away from my house, one street over.

"We're almost neighbors," I said, with a friendly smile. I could understand why Kirk wasn't fond of this guy. "We're on Pilgrim Way, near the river."

"Huh? Sure." Looking preoccupied, Eddie slipped his card back in his wallet and sauntered off. As he headed for the door, he nearly bumped into Kirk Schiffer, my best friend's husband, who'd just come in.

Kirk gave Eddie the most un-Kirk-like scowl I'd ever seen.

"Watch where you're going, Eddie. Nice that you're able to lounge around town, while the staff at BlueSurf are putting in overtime to make up for a year of your mistakes." His loud, angry tone caught the attention of nearly everyone in the bakery. Beck shot me a wide-eyed look from the espresso machine. It shocked both of us. This was not the Kirk we knew.

He approached the counter, and I saw deeper lines etched in his forehead, shadows under his eyes. He was dressed in a suit and buttoned-down shirt, like he'd just come from a work meeting at his software startup in Santa Cruz.

I leaned over the counter and lowered my voice.

"Kirk, are you okay?"

Kirk blinked and looked around him, as if suddenly realizing where he was—a public place. He rubbed his face with his hand.

"I'm sorry about that, Gracie. It's been a hell of a day." He shook his head. "I know it's last minute, but are you still taking orders for Valentine's Day?"

"As long as it's something on our holiday menu," I said warily, glancing at the clock. "What do you need?"

I noticed how bloodshot his eyes were. "BlueSurf is launching Tsunami, our biggest product, and I lost track of time. I haven't gotten anything for Elana. *Please* don't tell her this." He looked at the placard on the display case, which had photos of our special holiday items. The expression on his face was pleading. "You know her, Gracie. What does she want?"

Obviously, Kirk was in a stressful situation at work, but this was kind of a cop-out. From my previous life working in tech, I knew how crazy product launches could be. But if you're married to someone like Elana—for whom Valentine's Day is a *huge* deal—you'd better mark your calendar and think ahead.

Thinking about my recent conversations with Elana, I knew what she wanted. This was easy. It wasn't something at the Laughing Loaf. She'd sent me a photo. But I looked at the line forming behind Kirk. I had to wrap this up quickly.

I leaned over the counter. "She wants a pink sequin designer jacket at Nordstrom. Once we close, I'll send you the pic she sent me. Also, you know how much she loves chocolate. Get her a box of the raspberry chocolate beignets while she's waiting for the jacket."

Kirk's face softened with relief. It was hard to believe this was the same man who had lashed out at his employee just five minutes ago. "A box of raspberry chocolate beignets. Perfect." He looked down at his phone and scrolled with his finger. The corners of his mouth turned up wryly. "Uh, she sent me a picture of that jacket two weeks ago, sooo—" He looked back and forth between the photo on his phone and me. "I'm good. I owe you, Gracie. Can I pick those up when you open tomorrow morning? I can give her the beignets for breakfast before she leaves for work."

"We'll have those for you. But get here right when we open at 7. It'll be busy."

One of the last customers in line asked if we did custom layer cakes. An easy answer: no, our red velvet cupcakes were as close as we got. The final customer in line wanted a delivery of beignets and toaster pastries. Our young cupids would be thrilled to take on more deliveries.

After the last customer left, I locked the front door. Beck and Maeve, as we usually did after closing, had cranked up the music volume. I could feel the beat thumping in my chest. Maeve had introduced us to a playlist of Irish pop from the 80s and 90s. Beck and I were learning to bake to a whole new list of retro music.

We'd all be at The Laughing Loaf till early evening, making sure everything that could be baked in advance was ready for tomorrow, and everything prepped was set for baking or frying up in the morning.

"Gracie, the regular sourdough loaves and brioche are ready for their overnight rise in the fridge," Maeve said. "Once I put them in, I've got some time. Need help with anything else?"

Beck popped her head up from where she was working at the metal table. "I could use help mixing the red velvet cupcake batter." Maeve rolled a tray of sourdough boules over to the industrial fridge "I'll be right there."

Around 5 p.m., Sky Robbins—River Grove High's resident class clown—stuck his head in the back door of The Laughing Loaf, a crown of hearts tipped jauntily on his head. Sky was dressed in a cupid outfit he put together himself, consisting of white track shorts, a flesh-colored t-shirt, and a bright red quiver of plastic arrows. He wore a sash, beauty-contestant style, that said CUPID. On Sky's gangly, skinny frame, the look was comical. His delivery partner Dakota Li wore a bright pink jumpsuit with a banner that said I'M WITH CUPID, and white high tops.

"Gracie, Dakota and I are *ba-aaack*. Got any new orders?"

"How'd it go, you two?" I turned to him as I wrapped a tray of cherry scones I'd freeze for bake-up tomorrow.

"Speed Spot Motors was busy, but Jeanne Daniels took the order from us. She said it looked great. She gave us a big tip." Sky raised an eyebrow. "We're making the big bucks now." Dakota stood right behind him on the steps, her straight black hair waving like a sheet of silk as she nodded, talking to a friend on her cell phone. She turned around to snort with laughter when she heard him and immediately started telling her friend on the phone about it. She looked up and shouted back.

"Uh, hey—Sky? We're *splitting* that."

"Just know, not everyone's going to give you a tip, Sky." The wind whipping down the alley hit me and I shivered. "Come in from the cold, you two." I waved them in, checking the baking rack near the back door, where Beck and I had been stacking the wrapped Valentine's Day orders for delivery. At a post-Christmas brainstorming meeting, we'd come up with the idea of a Valentine week delivery service, employing some of the high schoolers who frequented the bakery in the mornings before school.

The high schoolers had come by around 4 p.m. to get their list of orders and then took off to deliver them. The deliveries had started Monday with just a few, then the number had increased today. The delivery service had gone off without a hitch so far—the young gang was thrilled to be doing it, and the feedback from those receiving the deliveries was overwhelmingly positive.

Tomorrow, on Valentine's Day, our delivery schedule was almost fully booked, with deliveries from 4 p.m. through 7 p.m. We'd even gotten several orders from out of town, from customers in Santa Cruz, Aptos, and Los Gatos. I was thankful to have enthusiastic high schoolers who had driver's licenses. When I'd floated the idea to the high schoolers at the bakery one morning before school, I'd received so many responses, I had to do interviews.

I pulled a pink cellophane wrapped basket off the shelf and handed it to Sky. "One more—for Beck's parents. Give yourself some time. You'll have a bit of a drive up to Charley's Grade."

Sky nodded confidently. "Oh, sure. I know where that is. I've got a shortcut—I can get us up there in ten minutes."

I frowned at him. "*Whoa*, Sky. There is no rush. This is a twisty road and a lot of it is one lane. Take your time and drive carefully." The last thing I wanted was an accident to mar the fun and excitement of our holiday delivery venture.

I picked up another delivery, a wrapped tray of toaster pastries and a cherry chocolate sourdough loaf. "This is for the Mortons, down on Great Branch Way by the river." Dakota took it from me. "It's Annie's surprise for Eric. He's working from home today, but Annie's watching out for the delivery. Make sure you give it to *her*.

"Got it, Gracie," Dakota said confidently. Anything else for today?"

"Nope, but tomorrow's going to be crazy. We had eighteen orders and several more came in right at closing. I'm still splitting them up between you guys and Jeb and Chloe. Any chance you can come a little earlier tomorrow?"

Sky did a deep bow with a flourish of his hand. "At your service, Ms. Markley. I'll be here at 3:30."

"I can, too," Dakota said. "I'll come here right after dance practice."

After the two of them took off, goodies in hand, I went back to my current batch of Cherry Chocolate Sourdough. I'd just blended in the sourdough starter and cocoa. Soon I'd begin the bulk rise, where I'd gradually fold in a massive amount of cherries and chocolate.

"I can't wait to hear what my parents think of the basket," The Laughing Loaf's assistant manager Beck Rodriguez said excitedly, as she mixed beignet dough for tomorrow. "They're not expecting anything, which will be *so* much fun." Beck smiled mischievously. She had added a few off-the-menu extras she'd made on her own, like pink sugar cookies in the shape of gingerbread men, one for each of her five older brothers, and a heart-shaped raspberry tart for her parents, cut in half, the two sides fitted next to each other in the box, each side embellished with heart-shaped sprinkles. If I had a child someday, I hoped they would be as devoted as Beck.

"Do your brothers do things like this, Beck?" I asked as I pulled the sourdough out of the proofer.

"My brothers come by the house to do things like fix the septic tank and clean up after storms," Beck said, as she began cutting the beignet dough. "When a tree blocked the road last year, my brothers chopped it up and removed it before road crews could even get there."

Life in River Grove in the Santa Cruz mountains had its benefits: the rural, wooded surroundings were gorgeous. Our town was nestled among the soaring redwoods and the beautiful San Luciano River. We were thirty miles from

Silicon Valley, but it couldn't feel farther from the business parks and busy expressways of San Jose.

The downside? Storms that brought road-blocking fallen trees and power outages that lasted for days. Rains brought the occasional mudslide and river flooding. In dry seasons, wildfires threatened the town, as winds drove them through the forest as if it were a pile of kindling.

Riverside Saloon owner and former mayor Reggie McFerrin had shown me once on a walk in the woods, that even the worst burned trees, given up as dead, survived these fires. Rings of tiny seedlings appeared after these fires, signs of hope after devastation.

Life after destruction, which confirmed that River Grove was the perfect place for me.

The road up to Beck's parents' house wound up high into the mountains, only one lane in parts. Just since I'd come to River Grove, the road had washed out twice. Her parents had to drive fifteen minutes out of their way, over a dirt road, to get to a road leading to downtown and civilization.

Beck dumped a bowl of washed raspberries into a pan on the stove, to make more filling for the beignets. "I'm glad my brothers are willing to do those things. But I'd rather bake."

I raised an eyebrow. "I'm with you."

Ten minutes later, Jeb Walker and Chloe Westerman came in the back door, finished with their deliveries. Jeb wore a red tie and a navy-blue suit. As if rebelling against Jeb's button-down look, Chloe wore jeans, a black t-shirt embellished with red hearts, and jagged angel wings on her back that made her look more goth than cupid. She was sporting a nose piercing, which her mother had allowed her to have, after much negotiation and the not-very-subtle disapproval of her grandfather, Police Chief Westerman.

Jeb looked at the baking rack, concern on his face. "Wait—that's it? I thought there'd be more to deliver."

"I gave Sky and Dakota the last orders for the day." Then I remembered Jeb and Sky's ongoing competition. The two, who'd grown up as close childhood friends, were wired very differently. Sky was class clown, and rarely took things seriously. Jeb took *everything* too seriously. Now the two struggled to be civil with each other. They had four more months together before graduation. In the fall they'd be heading for colleges on opposite coasts.

"You both had the same number of orders today," I said with a quiet sigh. "You and Chloe just happened to deliver yours faster."

By the look on Jeb's face, that news brightened his spirits. "We took care of the Santa Cruz order first, then came back for the River Grove deliveries. I plotted our route on my maps app. Zero time in traffic," he said with a smile of satisfaction.

"Well done." I nodded at the two teenagers. "Finish your homework tonight and get a good night's sleep. Tomorrow's going to be a *lot* busier."

My father, a retired physics professor, was going over to Jeb's house tonight for the student's second tutoring session. This was a good thing for many reasons: it gave my dad something to do, and he loved working with students again. I was thrilled to have him out of the house, so my boyfriend Nate and I could enjoy a quiet dinner without my father's constant presence. We'd decided tonight would be the best time for our Valentine's Day celebration. Nate was making dinner, and I'd made dessert. Tiramisu, Nate's favorite dessert, was chilling in the fridge.

"How's tutoring going, Jeb?"

His eyes lit up. "Your dad's great at explaining things. You know, physics isn't so bad."

A warmth filled me, as I thought about how energized my father was, now that he had something to do. For the almost two years we'd lived in River Grove, he'd continued doing odd bits of research, reading papers, and following the careers of former students and colleagues at the university in Seattle where he'd taught for thirty years. It had made me feel guilty.

After all, it was the situation with my ex that had caused us to relocate to River Grove.

Two years ago, I turned in my now ex-husband Ben Morrison for selling defense secrets, then testified against him in federal court. Afterwards, the federal witness protection program—WITSEC--relocated my father, me, and our little dog Biga, from urban Seattle to the small town of River Grove in the Northern California redwoods. My dad gave up his career, retiring early, so he could move with me, his only child, for a life under a new name in a new place. Sometimes I felt guilty that I'd caused him to give up his career.

"I'm glad, Jeb. He's enjoying teaching again."

Jeb excitedly began to explain the principles of velocity, which he'd worked on with my father last week. Chloe Westerman yawned loudly.

"Gracie, can I ask you something when you get a chance?" She looked at me with wide eyes. Then Beck called her over to the metal table where she was filling cupcake tins with rich red velvet cake batter. Chloe went over and the two began chatting. Chloe, who'd filled in to help at The Laughing Loaf many times, went to get an apron from the store room and began pouring batter into tins to help Beck. The two whispered and laughed before they finished up the trays and put them in the oven. Maeve came over and said something to Chloe, and they all giggled.

After a few excited points about momentum, Jeb wrapped up his explanation and looked over at the young women nervously.

"I guess I should get home and start in on my homework," Jeb said distractedly. "You wanted us back tomorrow at 3:30 p.m., right?"

"Yes—you've got at least nine deliveries tomorrow. There will be a few more. Get your maps app ready. You'll need it."

After Jeb left, Chloe finished up with Beck and came back to me.

"Oh my God, Jeb is *intense*." She rolled her eyes. "He needs to chill. I wanted to at least talk with people we delivered to. He said that would cut into our delivery time and slow us down."

I smiled in commiseration. "You probably know this by now. Jeb is a tightly wound guy. And you know he's always competing with Sky."

"I kept telling him today: *Bruh*, it's not a race." Chloe sighed and brushed her long blonde hair off her shoulder. As she flipped her hair back, I noticed she'd recently dyed the underside of her hair a bright purple. A sneaky way to embrace a little color without getting comments from grandpa. "I'm sure he's nice, but he's driving me crazy."

"One more day," I said with an encouraging smile. "Hang in there. You're doing a great job. Please tell Jeb—I told you that a little friendly chatting with the customers is a good thing."

"Yes. Thank you, Gracie," Chloe smiled. "Oh, and I

wanted to ask. I know it's late notice, but I wanted to send my grandfather something tomorrow. You know he's not eating sweets anymore."

I nodded. Before Christmas, the Chief had been informed by his doctor that he needed to lay off his favorite food group: sugar. Recently Beck or I had cooked up an egg on whole wheat toast for him when he'd come in for his weekday public safety meetings with Mayor C.

"Beck and I have been working on something—a pastry made of almond flour and natural sweetener. The closest thing we could get to a cinnamon roll."

"Really?" Chloe mouth turned up in a smile. "That sounds great. If it's okay, can I deliver it?"

"I don't see why not." I studied the young woman's face. She and her grandfather disagreed, openly and quite often with each other. I sensed that Chloe cared about her grandfather, who'd helped raise her. Yet at this stage in her young life, she was pushing for independence, judging by the nose piercing and the purple hair. Chief Westerman told me a few months ago that he was desperate to build a better relationship with his granddaughter before she went off to college. It looked like both of them wanted that. But with the stubbornness in their personalities, that could be tough.

"I'll talk to Beck. I think we could have something ready for you to take over before you go out for your deliveries."

Chloe reached out to give me a hug. "Thanks, Gracie. You're the best."

After finally finishing up at 5:45 p.m., I left Beck to close up the bakery so I could head home to prepare for Nate's and my romantic dinner.

My father wasn't expected at Jeb's till 6:30 p.m., so when I got home at 6, he was still home in his office. I heard the printer churning out sheets, so he was probably getting handouts ready.

"I'm back, Dad." I called, as I set down a box with two red velvet cupcakes, frosted with cream cheese frosting and silver sprinkles. I'd decorated them for him and his girlfriend Mary Jo. I'd wrapped them in a pink box, tied up with a silver ribbon. For most of my father's relationship with Mary Jo, I'd avoided her.

Now I realized how much she meant to my father, and I was working on building a friendship with her. She ran the Growing Affection plant nursery at the edge of town. Mary Jo was different than who I'd expected my dad to end up with, definitely very different than my mother, who'd passed away when I was fifteen. My reserved mother wore twin sets in tasteful, neutral colors and enjoyed spending time playing the classics on our baby grand in the living room. Mary Jo was loud, followed celebrity gossip religiously and smelled like cigarette smoke. Understandably, my dad wanted very badly for me to accept his girlfriend. Back in December, after I'd bruised my ribs in a very cold swim during high tides, she'd brought me soup and sat with me in the evenings as I recovered. She was a kind person and cared very much for my father. I was trying to deal with my feelings and build a relationship with her.

If it wasn't a smooth path to that relationship, it was entirely on my side.

Soon paws skittered frantically across the hardwood floor. Biga, my chihuahua mix pup, just realized I was home. He pounced on me, putting his front paws up on my leg, a look of desperation on his face.

"Did Papa pay any attention to you today?" I sat down on the sofa in the living room and Biga did an epic leap up onto the couch and began nuzzling my side, burrowing into my armpit until it tickled. "Okay, I missed you, too," I laughed as I pulled him up on my stomach and started scratching his back. There would be no way I could have handled him at the bakery today, though a long day away from him did make me miss him.

After today, I was afraid I'd fall asleep if I stayed in a reclining position. I got up and checked Biga's water and food, pouring a little more into his bowl before I got things ready for our dinner.

As I smoothed a white linen tablecloth over our dining room table, my dad emerged from his office, wearing a corduroy blazer and carrying his worn leather satchel from his professor days.

"Ready for class, I see." I hugged him and felt a sudden urge to cry. He looked so familiar, the very essence of my dad as long as I'd known him. He looked just like he had when he'd come home in the evenings from the University, smelling of books, paper, and the odd, industrial scents of the lab. His face beamed.

"Jeb is doing well with the material," he said proudly. "Since he showed interest, I thought I'd bring some supplementary materials on velocity."

"Jeb told me all about velocity today. I think you're his favorite teacher," I smiled. "He's really looking forward to tonight."

My dad turned pink and quickly brushed it off, since his reserved British self hadn't grown up to accept compliments any other way.

"Well, uh, the important thing is, he's making progress," he stammered. "I just hope that I'm giving him the knowledge sufficient for him to pass his AP test at the end of the year. I'm not accustomed to teaching at this level. High school physics is much more of an overview."

I laughed. "Come on, dad. You're loving this. I can see that."

He blushed again and turned his focus to the pink box on the table.

"Well, what is this now?" He picked it up and sniffed it.

"Red velvet cupcakes for you and your Valentine. Decorated just for you two. A little early, since it'll be busy at the bakery tomorrow."

"Can I open them?" He asked, even as he tried to slip the ribbon off the box.

"Of course. You told me you were going to drop by her place after tutoring, so I thought you could share these with her."

He opened the pink box. There was a cupcake for him, with a large pink sigma sign on it in frosting, in honor of his years as a physics professor, dusted with red sprinkles.

Mary Jo's cupcake had a red rose and a green leaf, a nod to her career as a plant nursery owner. It was dusted with silver sprinkles.

"Lovely, dear." He almost teared up. "I know this must be hard for you—"

"I'm getting to know Mary Jo." I said, firmly. "I told you I would."

He said it almost in a whisper. "Thank you."

After he left for Jeb's, I took a shower, then slipped on a long black dress. I set the table and put a bouquet of red roses in a vase, with rosemary I'd foraged from our backyard. I'd snagged the roses from Mayor C's yard, near downtown. They were the non-hybrid kind, the older strains, with that true, rich rose smell. With the addition of rosemary, the bouquet smelled rich and earthy, like a walk in a garden. I set out two candles, to live up to the advertised "candlelit dinner" I'd promised Nate when I'd invited him over.

I stepped back, satisfied.

I had no idea what Nate would bring for dinner. He promised he'd surprise me.

Nate and I had gotten to know each other over the past year, after he'd moved to River Grove with his brother Nico. Nate had moved with his brother in an attempt to get him away from a scandal Nico had been involved with in Los Angeles—one that involved an expensive set of missing diamond cufflinks. The move didn't help Nico, who'd been found dead one evening on the back step of The Laughing Loaf, poisoned. After Nico's killer was found, Nate and I cautiously began to spend time together. We hiked the woods in River Grove, where he pointed out the birds he photographed for a living.

Before Christmas, I took my first break from The Laughing Loaf, with Beck filling in, so we could have a getaway together in Sonoma County.

The relationship had to move slowly. Nate was nothing like my ex-husband, Ben, but after the devastation I'd experienced, I no longer trusted my judgement on men. One night, almost three years ago, I'd found lists of transactions on Ben's computer at our home in Seattle. The amounts were large and from banks in Russia, China and North Korea. I realized that the smart, handsome man I'd married right out of college was selling tech defense secrets. When I confronted Ben about it, he threatened to say that *I* had been involved in his scheme if I turned him in.

The next morning, to protect myself, I went to the FBI with the data I'd copied from his computer. He and his friend Kyle were arrested. After that, everything seemed to proceed at light speed. I testified in court, then me, my father, and my little dog were relocated to River Grove under witness protection to begin life in a very different place.

I looked forward to tonight with Nate. For one thing, our getaway to Sonoma had been one of the few times we'd had to be alone together. Now, tonight, my father would be out late, tutoring and then seeing Mary Jo. We could relax and enjoy each other without my father's kindly but not-needed presence.

I checked the tiramisu in the fridge. I resisted getting a spoon and digging in for a taste, then smoothing out the topping to cover it up. It smelled creamy and rich, with overtones of espresso.

At 6:30 p.m., I heard a knock on the door, then Nate cautiously opened the door and peeked in. "Are you ready for me?"

I met him at the door, which I then kicked shut behind him. He dropped his bags immediately and bent down to kiss me.

"Well, hello. You *are* ready." He let out a belly laugh, as I wrapped my arms around his neck.

We weren't graced with my dad's presence, but we did have Biga's. My little dog sat looking up with impatient disdain at our displays of affection. If he could roll his eyes, he would.

It didn't last long. Biga was happy to see me, but he adored Nate. And he really wanted to see what was in the bags Nate had brought. When he began nosing at the bags on the floor, Nate quickly picked them up.

"This is *not* for you, Biga." Nate set the bags down on the kitchen counter and began pulling plates from the cupboard. I was as curious as Biga.

"So what did you bring?" I reached out to take a look at a bag. He gave me a smile and pulled it out of my reach.

"Nuh-uh. You'll find out soon enough," he said, mysteriously. "You've been up since 4 a.m., Gracie. Go lay on the sofa. Put your feet up. When everything's ready, I'll let you know."

I wandered over to the sofa, still curious as heck as to what he was up to. Realizing Nate wasn't handing out samples, Biga let out a disgusted snort, gave up on the kitchen and settled in on the sofa, curling up by my feet. I must have fallen asleep, because suddenly Nate was next to me, calling my name.

"Dinner's on the table."

I wasn't sure if it was 7 p.m. or 11 p.m. I sat up and rubbed my eyes.

I headed to the table, almost tripping over Biga, while Nate guided me by the hand, laughing under his breath. "You really are tired. Maybe I should have let you sleep."

I stopped and gazed in awe at the table.

The spread included chips and a bowl of guacamole from Riverside Saloon—owner Reggie McFerrin's own recipe—to brussels sprouts and macaroni and cheese, and what looked like tri-tip that Nate had barbecued himself. Everything on the table was something I loved.

"Confession here. Reggie made everything but the tri-tip. I cranked up my outdoor grill for the first barbecue of the year."

I turned to him and gave him a hug. "I can't tell you how good this looks to me, especially since I didn't take time for lunch today."

"Of course you didn't," he said with raised eyebrows and a smirk. He pulled out a chair. "Now sit down and eat."

I'd just sat down and spread a napkin over my lap, when

Nate took out a bottle of pinot noir, one we'd both tasted and liked from our getaway to the wine country in December. He poured a glass for each of us.

I reached a hand across the table and touched his. "You remembered my love language—other people doing the cooking, not me."

He picked up my hand and squeezed it. "Of course. It was fun putting this together for you. Reggie was excited to be part of it. He kept giggling, while I waited for him to finish with it, saying 'Oh, she's going to love this.'"

I scooped up guacamole with a chip, then ate it in a gulp. "There's nothing as good as Reggie's guac. I was prepared for a fancy dinner—to go with the candlelight. This is *way* better."

"How did today go at The Laughing Loaf?" Virtuously, he skipped the guacamole and carb-y chips and took a helping of brussels sprouts and tri-tip. "How's the teen delivery brigade doing?"

I laughed between bites. I explained how things had gone today, with the goofy cupid, Sky, with his lead foot and Jeb's carefully optimized delivery routes. "They're a little competitive with each other, which I should have expected. But they're doing a good job. I've already gotten positive feedback on the deliveries. But I lectured them all today. I'm a little worried they'll drive too fast tomorrow, trying to get all the deliveries in."

"These kids know the roads better than we do, since they've grown up here," Nate nodded as he sliced into a hunk of tri-tip. "Smart to be cautious, though."

"This was all a bit of an experiment," I said, after I took a sip of wine and looked around the table to remind myself that there were other foods besides guacamole and chips. "I'll be happy to get back to normal after Valentine's Day.

We've baked more than any week so far—with the exception of Thanksgiving. I'm exhausted. Though I have to say, it's been fun working with the teenagers. Since the pandemic, people are used to having things delivered. I wonder if people will expect that from us now on."

"It's not a bad idea." Nate reached for his wine glass. "River Grove is spread over a pretty big area. It would be convenient for some people to have that service."

I stabbed a piece of tri-tip with my fork. "We'll see how this goes first."

Nate's phone pinged. He scrolled through a message. He looked amused, then a little scared.

"It's Mayor C. She sent the River Grove River Rats schedule. We have our first meeting and practice Saturday. She's starting us off with a training program. Running laps, weight training, calisthenics, batting and catching drills."

"Mayor C came into the bakery to order something for your kickoff meeting."

He shook his head. "I have a feeling it's going to be intense."

I shuddered, remembering the pressure Mayor Corinne Webster had put on me to join the team. "I'm so glad I got out of that one. I'm sure she's thrilled to have you."

"Well, we'll see." He laughed. "Our mayor has very high standards."

"Exactly why it's better for *you* to be on the team than me."

After we finished our wine and wrapped up the leftovers, I brought out dessert.

Nate's eyes got big when he saw the tray of tiramisu with its layers of mascarpone, whipped cream and lady fingers.

He looked at it in awe. He looked at me and gave me a

crooked smile. "Thank you for not putting glitter or all that Valentine stuff on it."

"I knew you'd like it better this way."

I cut us each a slice and passed him a piece on a plate. He took a bite and closed his eyes.

"Oh, *yeah*. This is the real thing. Tastes like the one I had in Venice years ago."

I'd had tiramisu in Venice, too, but it was with Ben. I wasn't going to bring it up.

Right now, I wanted to pretend I'd never been married to Ben. Yet weirdly, I was sitting here with this wonderful man in this sweet little town *because* I'd been married to a defense-secret-selling jerk. Life is strange like that. The good things sometimes come because of the bad things. How can you sort them out?

I took a bite of the dessert on my plate and realized that I was tired and way too full to eat more.

"Thank you, Gracie."

Nate reached out for my hand. His light blue eyes glowed. "When's your father getting back? How much time do we have?" He said it in an offhand way, but Nate was an open book. The look in his eyes was smoldering. Our chaperone was nowhere in sight.

"I'm not exactly sure. He tutors Jeb till 8:30 p.m.," I said, stifling a yawn. "Then he was going over to Mary Jo's."

He got up and pushed his chair back. "To the sofa, my love." It sounded dramatic and not subtle at all. I snickered at him. He laughed, then bent down and grabbed me around the waist and swung me in the direction of the sofa.

WE LAID DOWN, side-by-side, on the sofa, taking up all the room. I lay up against Nate and rested my head comfortably against his chest. Biga tried to jump up to join the party. When he saw we had no room and absolutely no interest in him, he let out a flurry of indignant snorts and skulked off to curl up on my dad's recliner.

Nate planted kisses down the side of my neck, then I felt his warm breath tickle my ear. That should have been arousing, but as I lay comfortably against his chest, it felt strangely soothing. I'd been awake since 3:30 a.m. I fought to keep my eyes open, but I must have given up.

The sound of a key in the front lock, three hours later, woke me up.

Like two teenagers, Nate and I scrambled to a seated position, as I smoothed my rumpled hair and made sure I was fully covered. I didn't need to take the trouble. My father came through the door oblivious to us, humming to himself. I glanced at the clock. 11:15 p.m.

"Hello, John," Nate said, smiling stiffly, like a babysitter who'd eaten all the cake in the fridge. "Welcome back."

My father had a big smile on his face and looked like he'd just won the lottery. He had a few disco glitter sprinkles in his moustache.

"Ah, you two." He stretched his arms out wide as if he were standing on a mountain top somewhere, like Julie Andrews, ready to twirl around and break out into song.

"Isn't love a wonderful thing?"

Chapter Two

I woke up at 3:30 a.m., a little groggy from the night before.

When I got up, Biga jumped down off my bed and headed for my father's room. This was not the day to have him at my workplace. It worked out that he didn't want to go anywhere this early anyway.

I had in the back of my mind that I should probably ask my father what had happened at Mary Jo's last night—the explanation for his euphoric "love is wonderful" greeting.

But I had way too much on my mind.

Today was the big day.

Maeve, Beck and I had a lot to do before we opened the doors to the high school regulars—who always kept us busy.

Since I was first in at the bakery, I made a pot of coffee in the coffee maker I'd gotten for the back room, which was our store of quick coffee-on-demand on busy days like this.

I poured myself a big cup, went to the fridge and poured a dollop of cream in it. I found a pop playlist and turned the sound system up loud. Fortified by caffeine and music, I got to work.

I checked loaves in the proofer and fridge, then mixed up cinnamon roll filling and the dough for the strawberry toaster pastries, which the high schoolers had fallen in love with. It seemed our homemade toaster pastries were nostalgic for both young and old customers.

I looked at the recipe Beck and I had been working on – for a sugar-free, healthier cinnamon roll for Chief Westerman. I'd mix up a small batch after lunch, so we'd have a few cinnamon rolls for Chloe to deliver to her grandfather.

Beck came in at 5:30 a.m., looking way cheerier and more awake than me.

"Happy Valentine's Day, Gracie!" She took off her down jacket and hung it up, then pulled her apron off the rack. "This is going to be fun. I've got something for you. I'll give it to you later when we're less busy."

I looked up from the toaster pastry dough I was rolling out.

"You didn't have to, Beck." I wondered if it was more baked goods, which honestly, after last night's feast, I didn't have much of an appetite for. On the other hand, Beck's track record for creating delicious new pastries at home was impressive.

"You and Sam doing anything special tonight?" I asked as she filled the large pot on the stove with oil for frying beignets.

"We never go out to dinner on Valentine's Day. Every place is so crowded. So Sam's bringing home takeout from a Mexican place we like in San Jose." She went back to pull the tub of beignet dough out of the fridge. "We'll probably watch a movie, or at least part of one. I always fall asleep early."

I told Beck the story of me falling asleep on Nate and not waking up till my dad got home.

Beck giggled.

"Not a very romantic evening then."

I snorted a laugh. "Not at all. But Nate did a dinner of all my favorite things, so it was great. Reggie's guacamole and chips and mac and cheese. And he grilled tri-tip."

"He knows how to make you happy." Beck laughed as she cut beignet dough into rectangles.

I looked over my list for the day. We had 26 orders to be filled and delivered this afternoon, but apart from the cherry chocolate sourdough, we'd be baking those later in the day so they'd be fresh. Much as I wanted my two delivery teams to drive safely and responsibly this afternoon, deliveries would have to be efficient to take on that many orders in three hours.

"Maeve's on bread duty, so she'll take care of that and pitch in anywhere else when needed." I scanned the list of orders.

"I've been teaching her the espresso machine, too," Beck said as she began spooning the chocolate raspberry mixture onto the beignet rectangles. "She has coffee experience from the bakery in Napa. If you and I need to be back here, she can take over at the counter."

"Very smart, Beck." I gave her an air high five.

Maeve had started filling in at The Laughing Loaf after my bruised ribs took me out of action in December. She'd just started a part-time job at a new bakery, Le Pain Parisienne in Napa, in the wine country. She baked on the weekends up north, then drove down to River Grove on Sunday nights to a room she rented at Mayor C's house during the week. After working the counter at a bakery in Sonoma, she was finally getting bread-baking experience at both of her places of employment. I was enjoying having the extra help with the bread and the company of another bread-obsessed person.

At 6 a.m., Maeve came in, carrying little boxes of Guinness cupcakes for us that she'd made at Mayor C's the night before. She hung up her coat and scarf, and filled her coffee mug at the coffeemaker.

"I had to be *really* quiet making these last night. I felt guilty even turning on the mixer. Do you know how early Mayor C goes to bed? 8:30 p.m!" Maeve carried her coffee back to the bread table. "Then she gets up at 4:30 a.m. to work out."

"That sounds like Corinne." I smiled. "You two are getting along?"

"We are. She acts tough, but she's quite sweet. Don't tell anybody," Maeve said in her Irish accent and laughed. "I don't think she wants people to know."

I wondered what the first River Grove River Rats practice would be like for Nate. Even if she was secretly nice, Mayor C had goals. And one of those goals was making sure River Grove's team was first in the league. Nate was in good shape, but I wondered how sore he'd be after practices.

"All right. Thirty minutes to opening. Maeve, you want to check the coffee bar and dining area?"

Maeve nodded.

"I'll check the restrooms and make sure the ladies' room door doesn't stick." After spells of rainy weather, the restroom doors tended to absorb moisture, swell up and stick. I'd been trapped inside for a few minutes on a busy day last year and Beck's cabinet maker husband had driven over to the bakery with his tool chest to unstick the door.

Five minutes before our opening of 7 a.m., the bakery smelled and looked amazing. Kirk Schiffer came to the back door and picked up the order for Elana, which I'd tucked a French chocolate bar into, as a special treat.

The back room tables were filled with trays of cinnamon rolls and sugar-dusted beignets. Boules of fresh bread lay on racks, ready for the display case. Tables in the dining room shone. The counter was ready, with a sign that listed our Valentine menu. I took out the joke of the day and set it out on its stand.

Valentine's Laughing Loaf Joke of the Day
Why didn't the skeleton want to send any
Valentine's Day cards?
His heart wasn't in it.

Teenagers, backpacks slung over their shoulders, were gathering outside in the cool, damp air. They chatted, punched each other, ran around each other and showed each other things on their phones. With their sense of humor, energy, and complete lack of filters, these young adults jumpstarted my day. It had taken me a while to appreciate them. Now I didn't know what I'd do if I didn't see them every weekday morning.

The Laughing Loaf was a stop for coffee, breakfast and last-minute homework time before they continued on to River Grove High School. They entered loudly, like a whirl-wind. And at 8:15 a.m., they barreled out the way they came in, rushing to get to school before the bell.

I opened the door and flipped the sign with its picture of a Laughing Loaf to OPEN.

And they poured in, saving places with their backpacks and purses at the coveted large round table in the dining area. Then the line formed at the counter, and our busy day began.

The display case was already filled with the teen favorite, French toast sticks, as well as cinnamon rolls and the tray of strawberry toaster pastries, which smelled of buttery, fruity goodness.

Beck was at the espresso machine, while I took orders. Maeve stayed in the back, prepping bread for baking, doing folds on the batches of sourdough, and tidying up our messes from the early morning.

Sky stood in line with Dakota, ready to order. He wore the standard down jacket with jeans and a flannel shirt.

"Gracie, give me two of those pop tart things and an Americano, room for cream."

"Both for you, huh?" I smiled. "Or are you sharing?"

"He is *not* sharing." Dakota smirked behind him. "He is really going to eat both. I've seen it happen."

Sky looked at us both with a look of innocent surprise. "But I'm a growing boy."

I plated the two pastries, and in a minute, handed him the Americano that Beck had just made.

Jeb was a few students after Sky. His buttoned-down shirt was perfectly pressed, and he wore a blazer, not a down jacket. He was giving off Dr. John Markley vibes.

I went to pull out the scone he wanted and nodded to Beck who was already preparing his latte.

"How did the tutoring session go last night?" I asked.

His face brightened. "Great. Your father told me about velocity. It was so cool. After he left, I looked up some of the experiments Einstein did."

I broke into a spontaneous smile. I was feeling a *little* self-congratulatory. This pairing had been one of my best ideas ever. My dad was back in his element—teaching. For the first time, Jeb seemed genuinely excited about a subject, not just the grade he'd get out of it.

"Great, Jeb." I handed him his latte and his scone on a plate. "I'm glad to hear it. I'll see you at 3:30 p.m."

A little before the students had to leave for the high school, a young man came inside and joined the line. It was hard to tell his age, since he was on the shorter side and looked youthful enough to be a high school student. He could just as easily be my age. His blond, spiky hair gave him a slightly countercultural look, like a young dude from the streets of Portland. He wore that look with flair; his jeans and fancy shoes gave him a more fashionable look than I remembered seeing in more casual Oregon.

"You're not a River Grove High Schooler, are you?" I asked. "You look young enough to be."

He laughed. "No, but that's flattering. My name's Ezra. I finished up my master's in software engineering and moved down here in the fall to work with a software company in Santa Cruz."

"Would the company be BlueSurf by any chance?"

He had an easy, almost flirtatious way about him. He smiled. "Yes, good guess. I interviewed with their CEO Kirk Schiffer last summer, and received a job offer a few weeks later."

I gave him his cappuccino and toaster pastry, and he immediately blended into the crowd of teenagers.

After the line at the counter died down, I went back to replenish the display case from the back. Beck had just set out a new fresh-from-the-hot-oil tray of golden-brown beignets that smelled richly of chocolate and raspberry.

The morning passed uneventfully. The bakery was always filled but it wasn't overwhelming. It was looking like we'd get through this day without too much stress. The deliveries were the only thing I still worried about. Setting four teenagers loose on River Grove's twisty roads and the inevitable traffic on Highway 17 and Highway 1 worried me. I wondered if I should have hired mature adults to take on the job. But these kids wanted to do this, were excited about the deliveries, and had proven themselves responsible.

By the end of the day, my worries didn't matter one bit.

What happened wasn't anything I could have expected.

By 2 p.m., when The Laughing Loaf closed to customers, Beck, Maeve and I finished up baking and arranging the delivery orders. The beautiful round boules of cherry chocolate sourdough looked stunning. We had one to spare, so I cut into the rich, chocolatey loaf and let Maeve and Beck have slices. And, of course, I took a slice—as a late lunch.

Beck took a bite and savored the flavor, before she continued wrapping a mug and boule in a basket with pink cellophane. "This is perfect. It's dessert and bread at the same time."

"Thanks for your work with the bread this week, Maeve." I smiled at the young red-haired woman. "Especially all those stretch and folds for the sourdough during the day. I'm liking your sourdough boules. The crumb is just right."

Maeve smiled shyly. "This is a great place to work. I know I don't have as much bread experience as you do, Gracie. Thanks for taking me on."

At 3:30 p.m., the teenaged delivery brigade arrived. Dakota, Sky and Jeb wore their outfits from the day before, but Chloe had upped her game. She wore a bright red t-shirt, a black bomber jacket and red plaid jeans. And a pair of heart-shaped sunglasses.

I pointed to the shelves by the door.

"Jeb and Chloe, your orders are on the top shelf. Dakota and Sky, yours are on the bottom two shelves. You've each got fifteen orders—each with an address and contact info." I stood in front of the four teenagers, my arms crossed. They were runners at the starting block, ready to take off as soon as I gave the word.

"I know you're all a little competitive with this. But take your time and stay focused. You're delivering treats that will make people feel special and loved. Please take the time to smile, greet the recipient and wish them a good day." At my words, Chloe looked vindicated, and Jeb looked surprised and a little puzzled.

"Obey the speed limit. Drive safely. And if you run into any trouble, you've all got my number on your phones. Text me when you've delivered your last order." I looked at Jeb and Chloe. "I've given you two the Santa Cruz and Aptos orders for efficiency's sake. There's some road work on Highway 1, but big surprise, when isn't there? You shouldn't have too much of a delay. Sky and Dakota, most of your orders are in River Grove, with a couple of them in Los Gatos. So why don't you go ahead and load up."

Chloe and Sky went out to pull their cars up to the bakery's back door.

Soon baskets, trays and cupcake boxes were loaded up. Cars started up and I heard them crunch over the gravel of the alley as they took off.

Beck, Maeve and I cleaned up after a long, crazy day, then began prepping for tomorrow's bakes.

As I loaded dishes and pans into the industrial dishwasher, I looked forward to receiving those texts that every order had been delivered.

And that everyone was headed home safely.

After prep was done, Beck, Maeve and I sat down at the metal baking table and devoured Maeve's Guinness cupcakes. They were moist and rich, and not overwhelmingly sweet. Beck went to her basket by the coat rack and pulled out a paper bag.

"I've been working on this for a while, Gracie. It's not a Valentine's Day gift. It just happened that I finished it this week at home."

She handed me the gift bag, an expectant look on her face.

Okay, this wasn't food. Then what was it? My curiosity was piqued.

Beck was watching me with a look of giddy expectation.

I pulled something hard and flat, wrapped in red tissue paper, out of the bag. Slowly I opened the tissue paper and gasped.

It was a small painting of the front of The Laughing Loaf. The classic structure of the original bank building, built in 1920, was visible, with the whitewashed siding and the front railing which had been restored right before we opened. Colorful abstract shapes of customers could be seen in the window. The Laughing Loaf sign hung on a wrought-iron hanger above the door, and a cartoon loaf of sandwich bread grinned from the Open sign on the windowed door.

And in front, I stood, holding my little dog.

All of this was painted in Beck's childlike, folk-art style. It was charming, whimsical. And perfect. I'd seen some of Beck's paintings when I'd visited her and Sam's house. This was so Beck.

My throat clenched, and I felt ready to cry.

Just a few months ago, I thought I'd have to leave the bakery, and River Grove, forever. But my father, Biga, and I

—and the Laughing Loaf Bakery—were still here. This picture was an affirmation of that. Despite threats from foreign governments and bumbling spies, despite a broken front window, smashed by two murderers, I was still here and so was this bakery, my new start in life.

"Thank you," I said hoarsely. I got up and gave her a hug. "It's beautiful."

She hugged me tight. "This place means so much to me, Gracie."

I looked around. Newcomer Maeve was looking at Beck and me, smiling faintly, though she must not understand what this gift meant to me. Come to think of it, Beck didn't fully understand either.

"Alright, then. Let's finish our prep." I stood up and carefully put the painting back in its tissue paper and bag. I stashed it in my tiny closet office.

Maeve put on a playlist of Irish pop hits, and we all got to work.

We were on the downside of this week's crazy work schedule. We started singing along to the Irish songs, which Beck and I were beginning to learn. We didn't talk much, just sang or hummed, as we passed each other on the way to the proofer, oven, and fridge.

I felt a sense of relief. We'd survived Valentine's Day.

I wouldn't feel completely at ease until I got the texts from all our cupids, that they'd finished their deliveries and were home safe.

Tomorrow would be a normal day, I told myself.

I locked up at 5 p.m., after Maeve and Beck had finished up and headed out. I took with me the bag with Beck's painting and some cupcakes and toaster pastries for me, my dad and Nate.

The Volkswagen bug was parked in front of our house,

meaning Mary Jo was here. I squelched the irritation rising up in me.

I sat in my car for a moment in the carport, talking myself out of my bad attitude. Mary Jo was a good person, someone who'd only ever shown me kindness. I would walk in, give her a toaster pastry, maybe even a hug.

I grabbed my bags and got out, and I strode purposefully toward my front door.

When I walked in, I heard a cacophony of sounds in the kitchen. My father was telling a story about getting in trouble in primary school in his small town growing up. Pots clanked against each other, probably my father rooting through them to find the right one. I heard sizzling and picked up the scent of seared steak. My mouth watered.

"This pot for the green beans, dear?" My father stopped his story to ask.

"No, you'll need to stir fry in the sauce, John. A wok would work better for this. Do you have one?"

"No, we don't have one of those," he said confidently.

I sighed. Then picked up Biga, who'd greeted me at the door.

As Biga licked my face, eager to see me after a day away from me, I walked into the kitchen. "We *do* have a wok—look in the cupboard above the fridge."

"Gracie!" Mary Jo smiled. She stepped away from her sizzling pan to give me a hug. "So good to see you. John and I are making dinner. Steak, stir-fried green beans and some rice pilaf. I hope you'll join us."

I'd just had a long, hard two days of work. What I really wanted to do was flee to my room with Biga and hide—put on some headphones and numb out to music like a moody twelve-year old.

The smell of those steaks wasn't going to let me.

"Okay," I said, furtively looking in the direction of my room. "I need to clean up and feed Biga."

"No rush. We've got things under control here." She cast an assessing look at my dad who was turning the wok over in his hands, trying to figure out how to use it. She smiled at me. "Give us about fifteen minutes."

I put some food in Biga's dish and refreshed his water. After he started eating, I went back to my room and flopped onto my bed.

He never helped mom cook. Why is he so into cooking with Mary Jo?

I was being whiny, and I knew it.

I hated the way I was thinking. My dad wanted so badly for me to like Mary Jo. She was important to him. I remembered the way he'd practically danced into the living room last night, proclaiming the joys of love.

My father had left his profession and his friends to move 900 miles away from urban Seattle to a tiny backwoods town, so he could be with his only child.

Now for the first time in seventeen years, he'd found someone who made him happy.

My father deserved to be happy.

What was my problem?

I took a shower and put on comfy sweatpants and a t-shirt, then went to spend some quality time with Biga. I took him outside to run around for a few minutes. In the twilight, he saw a squirrel running along the fence and barked to get my attention. He turned his head to look back at me, astounded at my complacency.

A squirrel! A threat to our safety and well-being! Are you going to let him get away with this?

I looked down at my phone to check my messages.

I was getting a little worried. It was 6:30 p.m., and I hadn't heard back from my cupids.

A text message popped up. Chloe Westerman.

> And DONE! Dropped off last basket in Aptos. Just getting home now.

I let out a sigh of relief. One more text, from Sky and Dakota, and I'd be able to relax after a busy, crazy week.

Biga had given up on the squirrel, so I jumped around the backyard in "play stance" to get him all excited. He started chasing me, pausing and leaping at me. We ran around for a good ten minutes, until my dad put his head out the back door and said dinner was on the table.

I herded Biga back inside.

My stomach growled as soon as I smelled the dinner spread. The steaks looked incredible, perfectly seared, and the salad and beans, which my dad had made, looked pretty good, too.

The kitchen clock read 6:45. Had Sky and Dakota finished and forgotten to text?

I had just pulled my chair out to sit down with my father and Mary Jo, when my phone rang.

It was Sky.

"Gracie," Sky said weakly. "We're at Eddie Sumner's house."

I stood back up and stepped away from the table to take the call. *What the heck?*

"Sky, what's going on? Are you guys okay?" I whispered urgently into the phone.

Someone was fumbling with the phone, then it sounded like it dropped. I heard Dakota Li's relatively calm voice.

"Gracie, I just called the police. When we came to drop off Eddie Sumner's gift, we found him in his garage. Dead."

Chapter Three

When I got to Eddie Sumner's house, the EMT van was parked at the curb. I heard the scratchy sound of one of the EMTs, whom I remembered was named Clint, talking on the radio. Chief Westerman had pulled up in the driveway in the RGPD car. Deputy Brad Castro stood outside on the house's front porch talking with Sky and Dakota.

I'd walked over since it was so close to my house.

The Chief stood at the opening to the garage. Behind him, amidst a collection of dusty furniture, moving boxes and power tools, I saw something covered with a sheet.

"Chief, I just got a call from Sky and Dakota."

The Chief nodded. He lowered his voice. "It could be an accident of some kind, but I think that's unlikely, judging by the circumstances."

Questions flooded my mind. As far as murder in River Grove was concerned, I had some experience.

"Why? How did he die?"

"Mr. Sumner was hit on the back of the head with a

heavy glass object. Some kind of award, it looks like. Judging by the wound, someone used it on him like a weapon."

"How long ago?"

The Chief shook his head. "I'm waiting for the medical examiner to show up. It looks recent." He looked at me. "Do you know this guy, Gracie? I can't say as I've met him."

"He came into the bakery yesterday, looking for a gift," I said, remembering Eddie's search for something to meet the minimum requirements as a Valentine's Day gift for his not-so-lucky girlfriend. I did know more about the man, since my best friend Elana Schiffer didn't always have the best boundaries when sharing about her husband's work conversations. Her husband Kirk didn't have a great working relationship with Eddie. And I'd seen evidence of that just yesterday: Kirk's angry tirade, directed at his employee.

I decided it was not my job to reveal this information, since I'd heard it secondhand.

"Is he new in town?" The Chief silenced a call on his phone. I noticed it was Mayor C's number.

Again, I wasn't the best source of info, though I knew he'd moved in last year. I'd seen the moving truck unloading when I was out on a walk with Biga one Saturday.

"He moved in last year—January, I think. It's just him living here, though I've seen someone else here off and on—maybe his girlfriend. He works at BlueSurf, Kirk Schiffer's software company in Santa Cruz."

The Chief raised an eyebrow. He chuckled. "I should have known you could fill me in, Gracie."

"I live a block away," I said defensively, feeling he was unfairly labeling me a nosy neighbor. "I run the town bakery, so I meet *everyone*."

As evening turned into night, it became chilly. I noticed Sky on the front steps in his cupid outfit, his thin, bony arms wrapped tightly around himself.

When Deputy Brad Castro finished his interview with the two teenagers, I went over to the porch.

"How are you guys doing?" I asked.

Dakota leaned against the porch railing, looking calm but tired. Sky clutched his bare legs, shivering. His expensive-looking high tops looked new and comically large on his thin frame. "You two had quite a shock. I'm sorry you had to see this."

"This was our last delivery." Dakota rubbed her eyes. "I pulled up to the curb, and we both ran up to the door with the basket. We knocked and no one answered. We waited for a minute or two, then knocked again. Right then we heard a screech of tires. I hadn't even noticed there was a car in the driveway. It took off and headed down the street."

"You didn't get a description of the driver? Model of car?"

Dakota shook her head. "I heard the screech and by the time I turned around, the car was gone. It was getting dark, so it was hard to see. I think it was a light color?"

Through this, Sky sat quietly, in his cupid shorts and tank top, quiver of arrows on his back. He looked at the two of us blankly. Sky wasn't usually short on words. He was notorious for his quips and jokes, which were quite entertaining on mornings before school at The Laughing Loaf. He was a life-of-the-party kind of guy. This new quiet concerned me.

"You okay, Sky?" I asked. "You look cold."

His attire wasn't suited for wet, cold February weather in the mountains.

Dakota studied Sky with concern then looked back at me. "Sky was the one who found Eddie. After the car sped off, we noticed the garage door was open. Sky went in and looked around and then he saw—."

Sky looked up at the two of us but didn't say anything.

"Hey, Dakota? Do you have anything in the car that might warm Sky up?"

She nodded and headed toward her car at the curb. "There might be something of my brother's in the back seat."

While she was looking, I sat down on the porch steps, next to Sky.

"You okay? That must have been hard to see."

Sky looked at me with that same blank face. "I-I didn't know what was going on at first. I wanted to help him up, like maybe he was just knocked out or fell. Then I touched his hand. It was creepy and limp." He turned to me with wide eyes. "I've never seen anything like that before."

While I was sitting with Sky, two cars pulled up to the curb in front of the house. A tall man wearing a navy-blue suit got out of one car. Leanne Robbins, a regular customer at the bakery, got out of her car and hurried up the front walkway to her son. She glanced over at the Chief and Brad, who stood by the open garage talking in low voices.

Both kids had called their parents, which was the right thing to do. I knew this situation wasn't my fault, but a wave of guilt washed over me as the parents walked toward me, worry on their faces. I'd sent their kids out to deliver for me, and they'd stumbled upon a murder scene.

Dakota got out of her car with a down jacket. She hugged her father and leaned into him as they walked up to the porch together. "Dad, thanks for coming."

I stood up to meet him. "I'm Gracie Markley, owner of The Laughing Loaf."

"Thompson Li, Dakota's father." He nodded curtly. I recognized the look from my years working in tech; he was a manager, someone intent on getting to the root of the problem. "Will somebody please tell me what happened here? My daughter said she and Sky found a man dead."

Dakota and I told the parents what we knew so far.

"Gracie, was this some kind of a random attack?" Leanne stood behind her son on the porch step. "This is just crazy. Things like this shouldn't happen in River Grove."

The medical examiner arrived and went into the garage while I was talking to the teens and their parents. I'd met Dr. Martin Ito briefly back in December when baker Daniel Bordleman died in front of The Laughing Loaf. He was young, around my age.

After he completed his examination, Dr. Ito came out and talked with the Chief for a few minutes. I stood near the RGPD squad car, while I called my dad to tell him what had happened.

I overheard much of the conversation between Martin Ito and the Chief, which had been my intention. Ito told the Chief that the blow to the head had killed Eddie, and that he'd most likely died between 5 p.m. and 7 p.m.

"The glass object was heavy, but someone used a lot of force to cause that wound." Dr. Ito lowered his voice. "It's very unlikely it was an accident, Dave."

The EMTs carried the stretcher into the garage, maneuvering around the furniture and boxes to get to Eddie.

Still worried about Sky, I called his parents' number. His father, Jim, answered.

"This is Gracie from The Laughing Loaf. Great, so Dakota dropped him off already. I wanted to apologize for the situation today. The Chief and Deputy Castro are trying to figure out what happened."

I heard a heavy sigh on the other end. "It's not your fault, Gracie. Yes, Sky is pretty upset right now. He won't talk. Dakota stayed for a while and sat with him. She wanted to make sure he was okay. She showed him some silly videos and got him to laugh."

"I've never seen Sky—well, speechless." Maybe I didn't feel guilty, but I did feel a sense of responsibility for these kids.

"Me, either," Jim Robbins said soberly. "This is a whole new territory for us."

I hung up and watched as the EMTs shut the back of their van and prepared to leave.

The Chief stood in the garage, looking around him and taking a few photos.

"A damn paperweight," he said, lifting a clear plastic bag in his gloved hands. The object inside looked like a large, clear rectangle. "And it killed a man."

"What does it say on it?" It looked familiar to me. I remembered seeing paperweights like this when I worked in tech. Usually they were awarded when an employee filed a patent or to commemorate a fifth- or tenth-year anniversary at a company.

The Chief held it up to the garage light above him. "Let's see. It says 'Eddie Sumner. For three years of service'. Issued this year."

He squinted at the print. "There's a wave symbol here. Then at the bottom it says—Kirk Schiffer CEO, BlueSurf. That would be the Schiffers up on Oceanview, right?"

A shiver went through me. I stared at the Chief and nodded.

Eddie Sumner had told me he was the "very important" lead architect of BlueSurf's new product.

Kirk had lashed out at him in front of a bakery full of customers My friend Elana had told me that Kirk and Eddie had a terrible working relationship.

That couldn't have been cause for murder, though.

Could it?

Chapter Four

Mary Jo's orange Volkswagen bug was still parked out front.

I came in the door of my house at 8:45 p.m.

Biga met me at the door, as if he'd been waiting there since I left.

It's bizarre how dogs sense these things—they know when we need them. When we're scared or feeling down. His tail wagged like crazy, and he put his paws up on my legs, wanting to be with me.

The lights were turned down low. My father and Mary Jo sat on the couch watching a British detective show.

When they saw me, Mary Jo stood up, concern on her face.

"How are those kids, Gracie?"

My father sat up and clicked the remote off. "We were worried. Tell us what happened."

I sat down on the recliner, and Biga jumped up on my lap. I told them about Sky finding Eddie. I didn't feel I should mention the BlueSurf connection. After all, I didn't know that was why Eddie'd been killed. I didn't want Kirk to be implicated in any way in his employee's death. Apart from today in the bakery, I knew him as a kind, reasonable man, a pretty good husband (despite an occasional complaint from Elana), and he made an incredible Sunday brunch. I couldn't imagine him doing anything like this.

"Are you hungry, Gracie?" Mary Jo headed for the kitchen. "Let me heat you up some dinner."

"Yes, I could eat." *Please, let it be the steak.*

After some clinking of dishes and a beep from the microwave, Mary Jo called me to the table. She set out a plate with steak, beans and pilaf.

"Thank you, Mary Jo." I looked up at her gratefully. "This looks wonderful."

"You mentioned the place—it's on Sunnyside, right?"

"Yeah, just a block over."

Mary Jo handed me a fork, a knife, and a napkin. "My friend, Carleen Fuller, does house cleaning for a man named Eddie on Sunnyside. He lives by himself, and he works for some high-tech company."

"That's him." I wonder if the Chief would talk to Carleen. A housekeeper might have noticed some things around the house.

I took my steak and ate the first bite. The flavor was amazing. Mary Jo was a good cook, though her repertoire was very different than mine. In a way, she'd continued teaching my dad to cook, after my few months of teaching him to cook for himself. That wasn't a bad thing. I'm sure he took instruction from her much better than from me.

I finished dinner after my father and Mary Jo had excused themselves and gone to the living room. Biga had stayed, and he looked up to me longingly; at this point, I was realistic. The love in his eyes was for the food on my plate, not me.

Mary Jo and my dad were now nestled together on the couch, her head on his shoulder.

I knew when I was a third wheel.

I took my plate into the kitchen, then excused myself to go to my room. Biga followed me.

My photographer boyfriend Nate was a creature of habit and routine. Just like birds instinctively fly south in the winter, Nate predictably texted or called at 9 p.m., Gracie time.

He'd been picking and assembling photos for a wildlife conservation fundraising campaign today. He was the only person I wanted to talk to right now.

I closed the door and flopped down onto my bed. Biga jumped up to join me, wedging his warm little body against my leg.

I went to text Nate and saw he'd already left me one.

Happy hearts day. Talk at 9?

Yes 

The guy called right on the dot.

"How are you? I heard about the murder this afternoon —and that your delivery team found the body."

"But how? I just got back a few minutes ago."

"Sam Rodriguez told me about it."

In River Grove, news of any kind circulated at a speed faster than any digital network. Sam Rodriguez—who was Beck's husband and Nate's next-door neighbor and friend— was good friends with Deputy Brad Castro.

"I'm as good as could be expected." I told him about Sky

finding Eddie Sumner's body. "I'm a little shaky. I felt bad for my two cupids having to see that. This was supposed to be a fun way for the students to make some pocket money. Now I'm worried about Sky. He could barely talk tonight."

"Does the Chief have any idea what happened?" The smooth, deep tone of his voice calmed me. It melted something frozen and immobilized in me from today's events.

"Dr. Ito, the medical examiner, said it was intentional, judging by the force used. Not an accident. The weapon was a heavy glass paperweight—a gift from his employer, BlueSurf."

"Wait—as in Kirk Schiffer's startup?"

"Yep." I told Nate about Kirk's interaction with Eddie at the bakery.

"I can't imagine Kirk doing something like that. I've only known him for less than a year, but he seems like too chill of a guy."

"That's what I thought," I said through a long yawn, the result of an even earlier morning at the bakery than usual. "Though when I saw Kirk yesterday, he said the product launch this week has been crazy. The Chief and Brad just started the investigation. Still it makes me nervous to even think of him as a suspect."

"Elana's probably in a pretty bad place. I'm sorry, Gracie."

"Thanks for listening," I said, trying hard not to yawn. "I was hoping to hear your voice tonight."

"Would it cheer you up to see a really weird photo of a bird?" Nate asked, after a pause. "I found it going through my shoots today. This one's from what I call my bird blooper reel."

My boyfriend, who made his living photographing birds, was a bird nerd—obsessed with birds of all kinds.

Nerd is a word usually associated with techy types, but a nerd is also someone who loves something obsessively and doesn't care who knows it.

I've been surrounded by nerds all my life. My father was a physics nerd; my mother, a music nerd. Nerds aren't trying to impress anyone with what they're into. They love it with an almost religious devotion.

Their love for it spills out to those around them. You learn something by just being with them.

I smiled affectionately as I leaned back into my pillow. "Bring it on, my love."

A few seconds later, I received a photo of a long-beaked bird turning his head to the side and glaring at the camera, his yellow eyes wide and his feathery brow furrowed. The bird looked very pissed off.

I snickered. "Why is this guy so mad?"

"Maybe he's upset that his girlfriend fell *asleep* on their pre-Valentine's date," he said with a challenge in his voice. "But it's not like I can relate or anything."

"So are you asking me for a make-up session?"

His voice turned deep and smooth like a late-night jazz radio DJ. He knew that voice worked on me. "Maybe I *am*."

I thought about the rest of my week. "We could do Saturday night. My dad and Mary Jo have tickets for a play in San Jose."

"That works. I've got the first practice for River Grove River Rats softball that day. Unless Mayor C goes full drill sergeant on us, I should be okay."

"Sure that's a good idea? We both know what she's capable of."

Talking to Nate and hearing my dog snore peacefully next to me gave me some normality after the shock of today's events.

"I'm feeling better now," I said with a sigh. "Angry bird helped."

I just hoped that Sky recovered from his experience this week.

I hoped that somehow Dr. Ito's assessment was mistaken: this wasn't another murder in River Grove.

Just a freak accident.

Chapter Five

At 4:30 a.m., I woke up feeling rested and relaxed. I stretched my feet out, curled my toes, and sat up in bed.

Then my stomach sank, as I remembered what happened last night.

I got dressed, pulled a clean Laughing Loaf apron out of my yet-to-be folded laundry basket and got Biga ready to go to the bakery with me. He leaped off the bed as I went to get his crate.

He hopped right in the crate himself. He'd missed going to the bakery with me.

We went out into the cold, pre-dawn morning. I could see my breath as I opened the car door and slid his crate into the back seat.

Since it was so close, I wanted to see if Eddie Sumner's house was shut up. I wouldn't be surprised if the Chief and Brad were there late last night.

I rounded the corner onto Sunnyside Avenue and looked for Eddie's house on the left-hand side of the street.

When I saw the lights on in his house, I actually pulled over to the curb.

Were the Chief and Brad—or maybe the Crime Scene team—up this late doing a search? Maybe they'd come over here to get an early start on the case.

I scanned the curb on both sides for the RGPD squad car or even Brad's truck. There was no one within 500 feet of Eddie's house. With the exception of a broken down 70s sedan with a missing wheel that had been sitting on Sunnyside for as long as I'd lived in River Grove.

Yet the lights at Eddie's house were on. And I swore I saw a figure moving behind the curtains and shades. A thin figure, short. It looked about the height and weight of Eddie himself.

I watched as the shadow continued passing back and forth. I even heard the noise of a piece of heavy furniture being moved across the floor.

I didn't see the squad car, but I decided it had to be Crime Scene. Or RGPD's own, searching for whatever they could find. Though it was certainly a strange time to do it.

Who else could it be?

I continued on to The Laughing Loaf, pulling into the gravel-covered alley with a crunch.

When I took Biga out and snapped on his leash, he tugged on it, nearly standing upright, as he made a beeline for the steps.

I'd ask the Chief this morning about the search. Maybe they'd discovered something that had kept them looking for clues into the morning. Maybe this would be one of those rare cases in River Grove that was solved within the day.

I switched on all the lights in the bakery, locked the door, and immediately put on a familiar pop playlist. I got to work.

No matter what I had going on in my life, diving into the morning bakery routine always centered me. I felt calmer as I checked the proofer and fridge to see rising dough was on track, made the rounds of the back room to make sure everything was ready for us to open at 7 a.m. When Beck came in at 5:30 a.m., she cut the beignet dough, filled the chocolate ones, and began frying. When Maeve arrived at 6 a.m., she took over on breads.

We had some leftovers from the Valentine's Day items, so I laid them out in trays and set them in a special section in the display case. Toaster pastries, red velvet cupcakes, a half a dozen raspberry tarts. I'd price them as day-old goods —cheap. The teenagers would devour them.

I hoped to see Sky and Dakota this morning. Maybe a night's sleep had helped Sky.

I set out the joke of the day on its stand. I chose a science-themed one, in honor of my dad and his tutor-ee, Jeb.

Laughing Loaf Joke of the Day
Why should you not trust an atom?
Because they make up everything.

At 7 a.m., I opened the front door to the teenagers. Our quiet time ended as they poured in, dropped their book-filled backpacks on the tables with thuds, and scrambled into line at the counter to order.

I spotted Dakota at the back of the line, talking with friends. Jeb had already found a spot by himself. His head was bent down over a textbook.

Sky was nowhere to be seen.

When Dakota got to the counter, I took her order and asked if she'd heard anything from Sky.

"I hung out with him at his house after I dropped him off last night. We played a video game, but he didn't even want to finish it. Said he was tired and just wanted to go to bed."

"Is that normal for him?"

Dakota shook her head. "Sky's always up for fun. What he saw yesterday really bothered him."

"I'm sure it did."

I frowned. Seeing something like that for the first time must have been tough—it could take Sky a while to get over this. I wondered if it would help for Sky to talk to someone about this. When a friend of mine up in Washington hit and seriously injured a jaywalker, she'd been contacted by a police counselor who talked through the event with her. It had helped her process the experience.

Mayor C and the Chief came in around 8:30, taking their coffee and breakfast over to the corner table. After they were seated, I brought out an egg on whole wheat bread that Maeve had made up for him in the back room. It wasn't the sweet treat that he used to have at The Laughing Loaf, but it was really good bread.

"This is from Maeve, who says enjoy your breakfast." I set it down next to his coffee.

"Tell her thank you, Gracie," the Chief said, as he eyed it with excitement. "And Chloe brought me the low-carb cinnamon roll you made for me yesterday. It wasn't what I'm used to, but you know, it wasn't half bad."

The Chief might be damning us with faint praise—but I understood what he meant and sympathized with him. It's hard to make changes to your diet. Substitutes try to trick you into thinking you're eating the real thing, but your body knows the cold truth—you're not.

"I'm glad, Chief. Looks like you or the Crime Scene

team was up pretty early at the Sumner house this morning."

The Chief set down his fork and looked up at me, puzzled.

"Gracie, what the hell are you talking about? Brad and I left last night at about 10 p.m. And the crime scene team won't be there for another hour."

"When I drove past on my way here this morning, the lights were on, and somebody was moving things inside the house. Around 4:30 a.m." A sick feeling formed in my stomach. Who could have been there? Then I remembered what Eddie had said about his girlfriend.

"When Eddie was in the bakery the day before Valentine's Day, he said his girlfriend spent a lot of time at his house. Apparently, she didn't like her roommates."

The Chief and Mayor C locked eyes with each other. "I have some calls to make, Gracie."

Since he hadn't eaten his egg on toast, I took it to the counter and packaged it in a to-go container.

By the time I returned to his table with it, he'd collected his notebook, tablet, and coffee and was ready to go back to City Hall.

"Chief, can I talk to you sometime this afternoon? I have a question for you."

The Chief looked barely aware of my presence. He looked worried.

"He's busy, Gracie," the mayor said dismissively. "Can't you see?"

The Chief turned to Mayor C and put up a hand. "Now hold on, Corinne. Gracie, come to my office after you close. Then we can talk."

I was happy to see that the teenagers and some adults had cleared out our leftover Valentine's Day treats. While Maeve mixed batches of brioche and sourdough for tomorrow, I talked with Beck about making changes to our offerings based on what had been big hits this week.

I pulled up a chair to the metal table where she was mixing beignet dough for tomorrow's batches.

"Toaster pastries were popular with just about everyone," I said, and Beck nodded as she put a ball of dough down on the floured table for rolling out. "I'd like to make them a regular menu item. They're nostalgic. They said what we made was way better than what you could get in boxes at the grocery store. Let's think about some new flavors. I think we've both got some ideas on what would work well."

Maeve looked up from shaping sourdough loaves on one of the tables. "The strawberry ones were delicious. You can't go wrong with that. I'd love to see blueberry, too."

"How about chocolate hazelnut?" Beck began rolling out the dough into sheets. "First of all, it's chocolate. And who doesn't like Nutella?"

"Yeah, that would go over with the adults, too. I was thinking of trying to do orange vanilla—like a Creamsicle. Might as well go all the way with appealing to their childhood memories."

"I like that idea." Beck smiled. Then as she pressed the rolling pin into the dough, her smile faded into a frown. "Gracie, it was weird not to have Sky there with the other students this morning. I mean, he's a regular."

It did feel off today, without Sky. Among the teenagers, where there could be some drama, Sky was a lighthearted presence. He never took himself too seriously, and he always made us and his peers laugh.

"I'm going to check in with his mom this afternoon and see how he's doing. I want to ask the Chief some questions, too."

On my lunch break, I put on Biga's harness and leash and took him out for a brief hike. As soon as Biga had seen the leash, he circled the pen, beside himself.

I thought you'd forgotten about me!

We walked in the direction of Eddie Sumner's house, crossing the street and heading for the path along the river. I was a little obsessed right now, true. At this point, the crime scene team had already been there—and maybe were still there, searching the garage and house for evidence of anyone who'd been there.

I turned onto Sunnyside from the path and quickly darted out of the path of two kids on bikes, pulling Biga to get him out of the way. Biga was, of course, outraged at the cyclists and continued barking at them until they were long gone down the path.

The street looked deserted today. Sunnyside looked very much like my street, Pilgrim Way. A few of the houses were older, built as cabins or bungalows in the 1960s and 1970s; some like ours, had been remodeled and additions had been built on. The rest of the homes were new, ranch-style homes, erected on empty lots or where older homes had been torn down. Eddie's was one of the new homes—a white, fake-Craftsman-style house with grey shutters, a bright purple front door surrounded by glass panels, and a large garage, now closed. There was no backyard fence, so I could see the backyard, overgrown with weeds and unkempt rose bushes. In the overgrowth, I saw a children's playhouse, built to look like a small model of the Craftsman-style house.

As I approached the street, I saw a silver sports coupe parked in front.

Of course, I kept walking—toward it.

A young woman with long, dark straight hair sat in the car, looking down at her phone. She had her window open. She was fashion-model thin. Her face was pale, but her makeup, down to her false eyelashes, looked perfectly applied.

"Hi, can I help you?" I asked, with what I thought was a friendly smile. "Are you lost?"

To say she looked startled was a bit of an understatement. She stammered when she looked up at me. "N-no. I just came here to—that is, my boyfriend died here last night."

"You're Eddie's girlfriend. I am so sorry." I noticed the inside of her car, which was filled with a full duffel bag, discarded energy drink cans and energy bar wrappers. And strangely what looked like a Prada handbag. The tech industry must be paying their employees better down here than in Seattle.

"Eddie came into my bakery yesterday to order something for you for Valentine's Day. My delivery team found him." I watched as her lower lip trembled.

"Oh, my God." She closed her eyes and shook her head. "Like, this is *unreal*. I was at work this morning when I got a call from somebody named Brad—said he was a deputy with the River Grove Police. He wanted me to come in and answer some questions. I'm headed there next. Oh—and I'm Laura."

"You're not from River Grove?" I asked, as Biga pulled on the leash, bored with this conversation. This was not the carefree jaunt around town he'd been expecting.

"I live and work in San Jose, but I usually come over

here and stay with Eddie. We met at my old job—when I worked for BlueSurf. Last night, I had to work late, so I missed our Valentine's Day get-together. I called and left him a message. When he didn't call back, I thought he was just mad at me."

The woman didn't seem overly emotional about her boyfriend's death. But then she'd just found out. And this was Eddie Sumner—not the gold standard as far as boyfriends go.

From what Eddie had said, this woman spent a lot of time at his house. Presumably she had the keys. I thought of the lights I'd seen at Eddie's house early this morning.

"You wouldn't happened to have come by his house early this morning? Like 4:30 a.m.?"

The woman looked taken aback. When she answered, her tone was testy. "I worked till midnight, then went to my apartment in San Jose. I slept in this morning because I was absolutely *exhausted*. Why are you asking me this? And who the hell are you anyway?"

"I'm Gracie. Gracie Markley." I shook my head as she started her car. "I live nearby, and I saw lights on at his house early this morning, that's all. Someone was in the house." Laura told me to mind my own business and spat out a word I'm not going to repeat. She cast a glance back at Eddie's house and pulled away from the curb.

AFTER COMING in the back entrance of The Laughing Loaf, I put Biga back in his pen. Before I went out to the front, I sat down in my closet-sized office to make a quick call to Leanne Robbins. She told me Sky had stayed home from school. He'd stayed in bed and wasn't even using his phone, which she said was a very big deal for him.

I tied on my apron and went up to the front counter. I saw the sun had finally fought its way out of the clouds. From the looks of the almost empty dining area, the sudden sunny weather had inspired customers to take their coffee and treats outside.

Maeve, who'd been manning the counter, turned to me, laughing. "The weather changes everything. It's maybe 48 degrees outside, and now everyone in town wants iced coffee."

I looked out the front windows to see a dozen sunglasses-wearing, down-jacket-bundled River Grovians huddled together at the tables.

I smiled at the sight of the customers, who shivered in the cold, despite the sun. "I think they're celebrating an end to the rain. I can't blame them."

When I locked the front door at 2 p.m., I left Beck and Maeve to finish prep for tomorrow. The two were singing together as they moved around the back room. I loved that with Maeve working during the week, I was able to offload many of my bread duties—which had always kept me to a very tight schedule. Maeve was happy to be doing it since her previous employer had kept her working the counter, not the bread-making area. Rafal, one of the bakers at Night Rose in Sonoma, had tutored her in bread-making basics after hours.

"Gracie, I've got all the loaves in the proofer and the fridge. Anything else you need me to do?" Maeve smiled. "I could mix the cinnamon roll dough for you."

"That's perfect. I need to go across the street to talk to the Chief." I thought about what else she might be able to help with. "First ask Beck if there's anything she needs help with—then mix up the rolls. But I'm betting with the weather. Tomorrow's supposed to be sunny. Let's make two batches instead of three."

"Got it, Gracie!"

Hoping the Chief still had time for me, I walked across the street to City Hall. Receptionist Peony Roberts wasn't at her desk, so I made my way down the hall to his office. He was on a phone call and sounded impatient.

"I know. You said you're busy this week, but I need to ask you some questions. If you won't come to me, I'll be coming to you."

I pulled up a chair in front of the Chief's desk. There was a box of something called "keto krackers" on his desk, next to a latte from The Laughing Loaf that he'd probably been sipping since this morning. Neither looked very appetizing.

The Chief ended his call and looked up at me, bags under his eyes.

"I was hoping you'd bring me one of those real cinnamon rolls," he said dismally.

I smiled. "I know. But then your doctor would find out. And you know how fast word travels around here."

"Good point." The Chief rolled his eyes. "So what can I do for you, Gracie?"

"I want to find out if there are any services or help available for Sky, the young man who found Eddie's body yesterday."

"You mean, like a chaplain or something?" He leaned back in his chair and thought about this. "I'm sorry about the kid and what he saw. But RGPD is too small for that."

"There aren't any services available? Anyone he can talk to? The Robbins don't have a lot of money. There's got to be some help we can get for Sky. He's struggling with this."

The look on the Chief's face told me he had a lot going on today and that this wasn't on his list.

"No, there isn't. Don't know what to tell you, Gracie." He threw up his hands and looked like he was preparing to go back to work.

"So there is no access to counseling services? What if you or Brad needed to talk to someone?"

The Chief grunted. "In that unlikely event, I'd pay for it out of the budget. Hasn't happened since I've been here, though." He gave me a look of self-satisfaction.

"Chief, so you *are* the one in charge of the budget. If any money is there for it—why can't that be used for Sky Robbins? Some kid who stumbled onto a crime scene? Isn't River Grove PD supposed to *serve and protect* River Grove?"

The Chief looked at me from under his heavily lidded eyes. He raised a hand in a gesture of helplessness.

"How much counseling time are we talking about?"

I shook my head. "I don't know what the follow-up would be like. But the kid didn't go to school today and hasn't been the same since he saw the body last night. He needs someone to talk to."

The Chief typed something on his keyboard. "There's supposed to be a local guy that we can call if we need him. Some young guy—Mark and Lisa Gordon's kid, Seth. They live up on Vista Park. He got a counseling degree at Santa Clara University. I need to find the right paperwork, then I'll talk to Leanne and her husband about getting Sky seen."

"Today or tomorrow?" I wanted to make sure I pinned him down.

The Chief groaned. "C'mon, Gracie. I've got a lot on my plate."

"Today or tomorrow?" I repeated, leaning forward in my chair. "And you'll talk to the Robbins?"

"I'll do it *today*." He gestured at the pile of papers and envelopes on his desk. "Are you happy now?"

"I am. Thank you, Chief." I got up from my seat. "Oh, did you know Eddie had a housecleaner? It might be helpful to talk to her. Her name's Carleen Fuller."

The Chief looked at me suspiciously. "And how do you know this?"

"My father's girlfriend told me. She's friends with Carleen."

"Yes, I know Carleen." The Chief grimaced. He sighed heavily. "John and Mary Jo are back together? Last I heard, they broke up."

"Nope. Back together and going strong." I tried keep a smile on my face.

The Chief chuckled. "Hard to keep up with these things. Well, good for him. She's a good woman."

"By the way, who were you talking to when I walked in? You threatened to come after them if they didn't come in for questioning."

The Chief leaned back in his chair. He rubbed his face and sighed.

"That was Kirk Schiffer. His fingerprints were on the paperweight that killed Eddie."

Chapter Six

I walked back across the highway to my bakery, my heart pounding. Of course, Kirk's fingerprints would be on the paperweight because he'd originally presented the award to Eddie Sumner.

As I thought about it, I started to calm down. Just because my best friend's husband had a hard time getting along with Eddie Sumner, BlueSurf's lead programmer, didn't mean he'd killed him. I'd talked with the guy for less than five minutes two days ago, and I could tell that I didn't like him.

But from the way the Chief had talked about it, it sounded like Kirk Schiffer had resisted being questioned. That was the part that surprised me.

Maeve had left, and Beck was almost ready to lock up at The Laughing Loaf, when I came in the back entrance. My dog was whimpering and had his paws up on the fence of his pen.

"Hey, Biga boy." I went over to scratch his head and give him a snuggle. "You've had a long day. Wanna head for home?"

Beck had just loaded up her wicker egg basket with a wrapped loaf of our day-old sourdough.

"He was not happy that you left. He calmed down, though—at least until *now*."

I pulled out his crate and lifted him over the side of the pen, as he nuzzled me and licked residual flour off my hands.

"Thanks for keeping an eye on him, Beck. Looks like everything's ready to go for tomorrow?"

I shut Biga in his crate.

"Maeve helped me prep all the tarts. And cinnamon roll dough is mixed and in the fridge." She smiled as Biga poked his nose against the crate's grate.

She paused for a moment and gave me a sly look. "Gracie, are you helping the Chief figure out who killed Eddie Sumner?"

"Oh, God, no!" I was surprised at the intensity of my reaction. "I went to ask the Chief to provide some help for Sky. Someone to talk to about what he saw at Eddie's. He's says he's going to do it."

"Thank God." Beck sighed and put her hand on her chest. "Chloe Westerman stopped by and told me she talked with Sky. He's having a hard time. She says he was barely able to talk." News traveled fast among River Grove's teens, too. I shouldn't have been surprised about that. I regularly heard rumors make the rounds within the 45 minutes the teenagers had with us before school.

"I hope he gets the help soon." I shoved a bag of dirty aprons into my tote bag to wash at home.

I left the bakery, regretting I'd ever come up with the idea to send the teens on their delivery mission.

Chapter Seven

Before I took Biga's crate out, I psyched myself up for going inside and facing my dad and Mary Jo. *Get in there. Be friendly, give her a hug, and deal with it.*

I carried Biga's crate inside, set it down and let him run free. He went in the direction of food. Mary Jo and my dad were eating takeout burgers at the dining room table.

"Gracie!" Mary Jo set down her burger and smiled at me from the table. "Did you get my text? I asked if you were up for joining us—and if you wanted anything from Burger Stop."

My dad wiped his mouth with his napkin. "I told her you usually get a garden burger and wedge fries." He got up and pulled out a chair. "Won't you join us, dear?"

What could I say to that? I gave Mary Jo a kind of half hug and took a seat.

"Sorry I missed your text, Mary Jo. I had a few things to wrap up at the bakery."

"No problem at all," Mary Jo said, patting my hand. "I hope you like what we got you."

The garden burger was delicious with layers of cheese, jalapenos, and avocado. I didn't need to be eating the fries, but what was I going to do? Push them away?

"How are your delivery kids doing today, Gracie?" Mary Jo asked, as she dipped a fry in ranch dressing.

I told her and my dad about asking the Chief to provide some counseling for Sky.

"The Chief agreed and is going to set that up," I said, then downed a spicy wedge fry, perfectly crispy on the outside and soft on the inside.

"I'm glad the young man will get some help." My father looked across the table at me. "Any news about the case?"

I hesitated. "It's early yet. The Chief and Brad have been doing interviews. The Chief's trying to get Kirk Schiffer to come in to talk to him—since of course, his fingerprints were on the BlueSurf paperweight. Then they talked to Eddie's girlfriend. I got to meet her at lunch time when I walked Biga past Eddie's house."

"My friend Carleen said she got a call from the Chief today," Mary Jo said. Probably thanks to *me*, since the Chief hadn't known she was Eddie's housecleaner. "She wasn't due to work on his house till tomorrow. She didn't like Eddie Sumner, though he did pay her well. He was very picky about what he let her clean."

I looked up from my burger. "He was?"

She nodded. "There were rooms in the house he wouldn't let her touch. She tried to organize some piles he had in his office, and he threatened to fire her."

Maybe Eddie had something to hide. Or he could just be a little fussy—someone who didn't want anyone to touch his stuff. My father could be that way, though less harsh.

"And it seemed odd to her?" I asked, as I realized this was one of the longest conversations I'd had with Mary Jo.

"Carleen's been doing this for years. She's cleaned houses for marijuana farmers, hoarders, and some pretty unhinged people." Mary Jo laughed. "Nothing fazes her."

It would be interesting to talk to Carleen and hear her views on Eddie Sumner. Maybe she'd seen things around the house that could have a bearing on his murder.

I stopped myself. It was fun to puzzle over this murder—to activate that part of my brain again. I was hoping desperately that Kirk Schiffer had nothing to do with it. But I had a busy life. I had a bakery to run—and now with Maeve and her bread-baking skills, I was also able to have a life outside it.

My dad and Mary Jo were talking about the play they were going to see Saturday night in San Jose. It sounded like a play my mother would have enjoyed, and I was surprised Mary Jo was interested in going. It didn't seem like her thing.

My father opened a bottle of ale and passed it to me. Then he looked over at Mary Jo with an admiring smile. "You'll have to tell Gracie about your days in the theatre."

"Oh, John." She chuckled and waved at him dismissively. "That was such a long time ago, it feels like another life."

Now I was curious. This new information didn't fit my picture of Mary Jo.

"You were an actress?" I finished the last fry in my basket and washed the saltiness down with a gulp of ale.

"I was in touring productions. Later I did some local theatre. It's a hard way to make a living, and maybe I didn't love it enough. Eventually I wanted to settle down. I met Bill at a performance in Santa Cruz, and he owned the local nursery. After we got married, I volunteered in community theatre. It was a relief to stay in one place after all that traveling. I fell in love with plants—and I fell in love with River Grove." She smiled, a distant look in her eyes.

What?

How did I not know this?

This was not the backstory I'd envisioned for Mary Jo.

I could continue to see Mary Jo as a stereotype—a gravelly-voiced, two-dimensional intruder who smelled of cigarette smoke and devoured celebrity gossip. Completely different from my proper, twin-set-wearing mother, who had died when I was fifteen.

But if I saw her as a living, breathing human being, with an interesting and unexpected past, I could maybe open up to her and accept her as my father's choice for a girlfriend. Even welcome her into the family.

And that was the fence I was teetering on.

I FaceTimed with Nate that night, a little sleepy, so our talk wasn't long. Nate was excited about the bird photos he'd chosen for the conservation campaign, and he'd just accepted another assignment, from the group who'd commissioned the coffee table book he'd done on Galapagos finches last fall.

Not that I was looking for it, but Nate passed on news he'd heard from Sam, who'd heard it from Deputy Brad Castro.

What I'd seen this morning as I passed Eddie's house wasn't an illusion. Someone *had* been in the house after Brad and the Chief had left the night of the murder. Furniture had been moved, and boxes in closets had disappeared.

Both the crime scene team and the Chief had left the house locked and deadbolted.

Yet there were no signs of a break-in.

Chapter Eight

On my way to work the next morning, I did the same detour as yesterday and turned onto Sunnyside Street. The street was dark, with only a few porch lights on.

As I approached Eddie's house, a faint light glowed behind curtains, in what looked like a bedroom at the front of the house. Thin lines of a figure moved behind the blinds in the living room as if someone were moving around in the room. As I remembered, Eddie had been relatively short—about the height of the figure I was seeing.

There were cars parked in the driveways of the surrounding houses, but there was no car in front of Eddie's house.

I pulled up at the curb on the opposite side of the street from Eddie's house and turned off my motor. I rolled my window down a couple of inches and sat back to listen. Most of what I heard was Biga scratching impatiently in his crate in the back seat.

I sat for about ten minutes, listening and watching the window.

Finally, the light went out. I watched, my eyes a little more accustomed to the darkness, looking for anyone leaving the house, but I saw no one.

Who—or what—was in Eddie Sumner's house?

I started my car and headed for the bakery.

When the high school students came into The Laughing Loaf at 7 a.m, I searched the line and the tables for Sky, but I didn't see him. Jeb ordered a latte, then sat by himself at a back table, and began poring over his physics book. After she received her coffee and cinnamon roll, Chloe Westerman walked over and sat down opposite Jeb. Without talking, she opened her binder and began reading through pages of notes. Maybe the two of them had gotten to know each other better during their deliveries, which was encouraging, given Chloe's frustration with the young man earlier this week.

When we had a brief lull, I went into the back room for trays of scones, tarts and cinnamon rolls to replenish the display case.

"Gracie, Sky's not here again." Beck's dark eyebrows arched and knit together like a concerned Disney princess as she laid out tarts on a tray. "I'm really starting to worry about him."

"I talked to the Chief and he's arranging for Sky to talk to a counselor—somebody from River Grove named Seth. Seth Gordon."

"Seth? I'm so glad!" Beck brightened. "The Gordons and my family are good friends. Seth's three years older than me. He's a cool guy. He'd be great for Sky to talk to."

Was there anyone in River Grove Beck *didn't* know?

"The Chief wasn't very excited about arranging this or paying for it. But he promised he'd do it."

I finished putting maple bacon scones on a tray, then

checked the doughs in the proofing unit and fridge. Maeve had to be up in Napa today for an event with Le Pain Parisienne, but she'd done all the bread prep last night, which made my job easier today.

"I hope it happens soon," Beck said.

When the Chief came in later this morning with Mayor C, I'd mention that I'd seen lights on at Eddie's house. I thought about what Nate had said, about there being evidence of someone in the house but no signs of a forced entry.

Then I wondered about Carleen Fuller, the cleaning lady. She probably had a key—or at least some way to get in to do her job while Eddie was down in Santa Cruz, working at BlueSurf.

After I'd stocked the display case, I went back to the counter. I looked out at the group of teenagers, their bags and purses strewn on the table around them. They were quieter than usual, many of them bent over books, notebooks, and tablets. I wondered how much that had to do with the fact that we'd just had another murder in town. And how much had to do with the fact that Sky, often the life of the party, was missing. Amazing what a difference the absence of one person can make.

When the Chief came up to the counter at 8:30 a.m., a tablet and large envelope under his arm, he looked prepared to meet me.

"I'll have you know," he said, a firm, slightly defensive look on his face. "I just put Seth Gordon in contact with the Robbins."

I almost smiled. He'd been afraid I'd bug him again.

"Great. Thanks, Dave." I leaned over the counter, lowering my voice. "I saw lights on at Eddie's again on my way into the bakery this morning. In the front bedroom. I pulled over to watch. Then the light switched off."

The Chief frowned. "Damn." He looked over at Mayor C, already set up at their usual corner table for their informal morning public safety meeting. "Laura Freitas surrendered her keys yesterday. Carleen Fuller's coming in this morning, and I'll get any keys she has."

The line behind the Chief began to grow. I looked over his head with a nod.

"Right, I gotta go. Looks like Brad and I need to do a stakeout."

As he moved on to the corner table, I had to admit the word *stakeout* sent a little thrill through me.

At lunch, I took Biga out of his pen and snapped on his leash. Clouds had cleared and patches of blue sky had opened up over River Grove. The sun chasers were still sitting at our front outside tables, but they were down to light jackets and long-sleeved shirts.

It was time for a refreshing walk on a beautiful day. Biga immediately sensed what was up. His tail wagged and he looked at me impatiently as I gave instructions to Beck before we left.

Now?

How about now?

[Withering look with narrowed eyes] Are we even still going?

My first instinct was to head for the trail that followed the river. But once outside, the sun felt so good, I decided to walk through downtown and over to Grove Park, site of June's River Grove Annual Chili Cookoff. We crossed the street and walked past City Hall and Spinetti's Sparkletown Cleaners.

Jeanne Daniels, co-owner of Speed Spot Motors with her husband Jake, was coming out of the door of the cleaners with an armful of plastic bagged winter coats when she called to me.

"Hey, you two!" She smiled down at my little dog, who drank up the attention like a water bowl on a hot summer day, his tail wagging like crazy. "I haven't seen you in ages, Gracie. We really enjoyed the Valentine treat delivery. Great idea getting the teenagers involved."

"It went well—that is, until the delivery to Eddie Sumner's house." I frowned.

Jeanne Daniel's face darkened. "So sad about Eddie. He was a regular customer. A little uptight about his car, but he brought it in for service right on the dot."

"Did you know him very well?" Biga sniffed Jeanne's feet for microscopic traces of food, then put his paws up on Jeanne's legs.

Jeanne shook her head, then looked down at Biga and smiled. "I knew more about his car than him."

"Nothing odd about his behavior?" I asked, tugging gently on Biga's leash and coaxing him to get off Jeanne.

Jeanne thought about it. "He was picky about things, but other than that, he was a good customer." She raised an eyebrow. "I know he worked for Kirk Schiffer at BlueSurf and the two of them didn't get along. People are saying that might have had something to do with Eddie's death." She looked at me as if asking a question.

I knew Kirk had gone through a hard time with Eddie and the release. But I liked Kirk, and my defensiveness was showing. Also, why would I know if Kirk had murdered Eddie?

"It sounds like they didn't have a great working relationship." I remembered their tense interaction at The

Laughing Loaf. "But that's rarely a cause for murder. If Kirk had a hard time working with him, he could let him go."

Jeanne readjusted the coats on her arm. "I guess. But I heard Kirk doesn't want to talk to the police. That sounds suspicious."

Kirk could be tied down at his office with BlueSurf's product release and the aftermath of his lead programmer being out of the picture. It's possible he wasn't avoiding being questioned at all.

If everyone in town was speculating about Kirk as a possible suspect in Eddie Sumner's murder, Elana must have heard it by now.

That couldn't feel good.

Chapter Nine

In Maeve's absence, I threw myself into the afternoon bread prep.

It felt good to mix up the batches, to knead and shape the soft smooth dough. I'd loved having Maeve to help, but I would always relish the process of making bread. It was an anchor for me. Watching it rise and develop a lovely crumb and heavenly smell filled me with a deep sense of satisfaction. Bread was—and will always be—my happy place.

Today I mixed up a small batch of rye dough, New York deli style. I'd been meaning to offer it as a special for a while now, for those few rye fans who asked me when it was coming back. I'd included it on our menu in the bakery's first year. The slightly grainy dough smelled earthy and rich—strangely ancient. My Saxon ancestors, back in medieval times, had brought it to England from their cold, damp climate, where rye grew better than wheat. Maybe there was some rye in my blood. I couldn't wait to smell and taste the results when I baked tomorrow.

"Gracie, you've been quiet all afternoon," Beck called

from the metal table where she was assembling apple tarts. "Is everything okay?"

"I can't get Eddie Sumner's murder out of my head." The problem-solving side of my brain was churning with what I'd seen and heard in the past day.

I slid the tub of rye into the proofer and closed the door. "Someone was in the house the night after the murder and then this morning when I passed by on my way in. The Chief said it wasn't him, Brad, or the crime scene team. Or Eddie's girlfriend, at least according to her." I told Beck about my run-in with Laura Freitas.

"Well, she must have a key." Beck said, as she laid apple slices into the tart shells. "You told me she practically lived at Eddie's house."

"But she handed her keys over to the Chief yesterday. And I saw someone in the house this morning. It's possible that Eddie's housecleaner, Carleen, has keys. Though she'll probably hand it over to the Chief today."

"What would people want in Eddie's house?" Beck asked as she wrapped a tray of tarts for tomorrow's bake. "Brad told Sam that whoever was in the house that night of the murder was pulling things out of closets, like they were looking for things."

"You'd think Eddie Sumner was an international jewel thief—" I said with a half laugh "—or a drug lord."

"Are you going to check Eddie's house tomorrow morning on the way to work?" Beck began filling another tray of tarts.

"C'mon, Beck." I smiled. "What do you think?"

After loading Biga into his crate, I left the bakery for the day, leaving Beck behind to do final setup for tomorrow at the front counter and lock up.

When I turned onto Pilgrim Way, there was no orange Volkswagen bug parked on the street in front of our house.

Once inside, I sprung my little dog from his crate, then filled his bowls with water and food. Biga scrambled to eat, and then as was his habit, oddly, he picked up pieces of his dry food and scattered them in the dining room. It did not feel great to step on the nuggets in bare feet. I have no idea why he did this. I wondered if it was a way of making sure he could eat with us. Like all dogs, he loved to eat. But he also loved being around people.

For dinner, I assembled a chicken salad with avocado, roma tomatoes, basil, and homemade sourdough croutons. My dad and I could have dinner together before he went over for his tutoring session with Jeb.

He came out of his study carrying the same worn leather professor satchel I remembered from Seattle. He wore a buttoned-down shirt, a tweed blazer, and jeans–the latter a concession to his new, more rural surroundings in River Grove.

Lately, there was something new about him, something I hadn't seen in a while. My father kind of... glowed. He looked younger than the man who'd sat in his recliner for the past two years, clinging to his past life by reading physics papers written by his former colleagues and students. He was doing what he loved again. Even though it had been his choice to leave his job and his life in Seattle, I'd felt guilty that going into witness protection with me had taken so much away from him.

Tears filled my eyes.

"Dad, you look great."

"We're continuing with a lesson on momentum tonight. I gave a preview to Jeb on Tuesday. He texted me that he's already gone over the materials and has some questions for me."

"You've got a devoted student there," I said with a smile as I laid out our salad plates. "And here I thought Jeb was only interested in business school."

"He might still go in that direction. I'm here to help him do well in his class and get his AP credits." My father tucked his napkin into his shirt and began to attack his salad.

"Ever thought about doing this for other kids?" I asked as I picked up a forkful of salad topped by a sourdough crouton. "Jeb graduates in June. You could put the word out to River Grove High School, maybe even to high schools in Santa Cruz and Los Gatos. You could help other kids."

My dad almost blushed. "Now, dear. Let's just wait and see how it goes with Jeb. I'm still learning how to work with high school students. It's quite different."

I wanted to roll my eyes. "Whatever. You should do this. You don't know how happy you've been looking lately."

He took a drink of his white wine then paused thoughtfully. "Gracie, thank you for sitting down to eat with us last night. It meant a lot to Mary Jo."

"I enjoyed it," I said, realizing as I said it that it was true. And that when I hadn't seen the orange bug in front of our house, my first instinct wasn't to celebrate. My thought had been: *So where's Mary Jo?*

It wasn't a huge development, but it was something.

After I finished cleaning up, I heard my phone ding. I saw a message from Elana.

I went back to my room, closed my door, and flopped down onto my bed. Biga joined me.

Elana's voice was hoarse, as if she'd been crying.

"Gracie, Kirk's a suspect in Eddie Sumner's murder. Even the clerks at the corner market asked me about it. How can the Chief think Kirk would do such a thing? Now with all the other things going on with the product launch, he has to deal with this?"

I tried to calm my friend down. "Elana, this is a formality. His fingerprints were on the paperweight used to kill Eddie. And, of course, they'd be on it. He gave it to Eddie. They just have to look into it."

Elana continued, in much the same tone. "Kirk didn't get along with Eddie." She paused for a moment, and I thought I heard some sniffling. "He's been really stressed this week with the Tsunami release. He told me he said some things to Eddie before he was killed." Elana's voice shook. She paused for a moment. "Some things that could be taken the wrong way."

"What did he say to Eddie?" Seeing how Kirk reacted to Eddie in the bakery, I wasn't surprised. "Did he tell you?"

"Eddie ended up in the position where he controlled whether or not the Tsunami product was released this week," Elana said. He " was constantly distracted. He'd already slipped on the deadline twice, so the product had been delayed six months. Eddie is—*was*—a brilliant programmer. Kirk admits he gave Eddie too much leeway. When Eddie threatened not to come through on the deadline this week, Kirk totally lost it."

I thought of the swagger Eddie had had when he'd come into the bakery and said he was the "lead programmer on a very important product launch."

"Did Kirk threaten him?" Biga crawled up next to me, and flopped his head down on my thigh, bringing with him an uncomfortably wet chew toy.

"He told Eddie if he didn't come through with the final version of the software this week, he'd be finished. He'd make sure Eddie never worked anywhere ever again."

"Eddie must have come through if the product was released this week."

"Just barely. He gave Kirk and the management team the scare of their lives."

I remembered how stressed he'd looked when he came into the bakery. His lead programmer was holding Blue-Surf's big new product release hostage. The hostility Kirk had shown Eddie was intense. Everyone in the bakery that day had seen the conflict between the two men.

"Someone heard what Kirk said to Eddie at work?"

Elana sighed. "Yeah. Most of the management team was sitting in the room next door when he said it."

I thought about this. Kirk's words could be interpreted as threatening to fire Eddie and give him a bad reference for future employment. Or they could be interpreted as a threat to finish him off, period.

Bad luck then that someone *actually* finished Eddie off.

"Elana, Kirk needs to do damage control *now*. The Chief thinks he's stalling because he's guilty."

I heard muffled sobbing. "I know, Gracie. But he's not doing it. And I can't make him."

I wanted to comfort my friend and tell her I couldn't imagine Kirk resorting to violence. That he couldn't possibly be a killer. That this was all going to work out, and Kirk would be in the clear.

But how did I know?

My ex-husband Ben, now in federal prison, had made several million dollars selling defense secrets behind my back for four years. I'd been clueless the whole time.

Something about that experience made me see that no one is immune to the impulse to steal, lie, or kill.

So I told my good friend that whatever happened, I'd be there for her. And we'd make a date to go to The Riverside Saloon, Elana's happy place, in the near future.

Meanwhile, I hoped Kirk had nothing to do with Eddie Sumner's murder.

Not long after I hung up with Elana, Nate texted at 9 p.m.

> Wanna talk?

Let me think. YES.

When he called, his voice was soothing and calm. I was still a little emotional about my chat with Elana but didn't feel I should share that with him. Instead I told Nate about my dinner with my father and his "glow."

"John's come to life in the past few months," Nate said. "Maybe it's the tutoring, maybe it's Mary Jo."

One huge development in Nate's and my relationship was that he now knew I was in witness protection—since he'd taken it upon himself to investigate my past with my ex-husband Ben by talking to a reporter who'd covered Ben's trial in Seattle. Nate had found out about Ben's sale of defense secrets, and how I'd testified against him in federal court.

Nate now knew my real identity, instead of the WITSEC bio I'd carefully memorized and repeated to him —while feeling guilty about lying to him the whole time. It was an incredible relief for me to be myself with him.

"My dad left everything in Seattle—his job, his friends —to be down here with me."

"Gracie, it was his choice. He seems to be enjoying his time in River Grove. Maybe with the tutoring and Mary Jo, he's found his place here. You know him better than I do, but since I met him, I've never really seen him unhappy. I can tell you he's *delighted* when he's beating me at chess." Nate chuckled.

I snorted. "It does seem to make him happy, doesn't it?"

"He sees me coming and runs for his chess set. I mean, it's ridiculous." Nate groaned.

"Well, at least you won't have to worry about that tomorrow night. He'll be with Mary Jo at the theatre."

Nate slipped into his smooth jazz DJ voice

"Oh, believe me. I'll have other things to focus on."

Calmer after talking to Nate, I let Biga out into the backyard to do his thing.

Then I got ready for bed and quickly fell asleep with my little dog curled up next to me.

Thoughts about Eddie Sumner's murder must have been percolating in my head because that night I had one of those very realistic dreams.

In the dream, I was driving to the bakery in the pre-dawn dark. As I neared Eddie's house, I saw lights on again. In fact, all windows in the house were lit up, and eerie shadows moved behind the shades. I heard the thump of boxes being moved and set down. Two people were arguing loudly, and I thought I heard the voice of Eddie Sumner himself—in the same swaggering, full-of-himself tone he'd used when he'd come to the bakery the day before Valentine's Day. The other voice sounded like the angry, explosive voice of Kirk Schiffer in the bakery last week.

Eddie was telling him to "leave his stuff alone." I woke up, sat up and looked around me, disoriented.

This wasn't real. You're in your bed, not on your way to work. And Eddie Sumner is dead. Definitely dead.

I flopped back onto my pillow, and after some tossing and turning, I went back to sleep.

Chapter Ten

I woke up when my alarm went off at 4:45 a.m.

Saturday mornings, without the influx of teenagers on their way to school, we opened at a more leisurely 8 a.m.

Even with the later time, Biga lifted his head wearily when I got up, then burrowed under the covers.

Somebody wanted his weekend sleep.

As I headed for The Laughing Loaf that morning at 5:30 a.m., I turned right onto Sunnyside. Most houses were dark. One or two had porch lights on. As I neared Eddie's house, I saw Deputy Brad Castro's white pickup, across the street from Eddie's and one house down. As my headlights highlighted the truck, I saw two heads silhouetted in the truck cab. I continued down the street without slowing down. The last thing I wanted to do is call attention to their stakeout. I could talk to the Chief about it later.

Unlike my noisy, crazy dream, Eddie's house was dark and perfectly still this morning.

Had the Chief and Brad seen any signs of an intruder in the house tonight?

I wonder who'd been in Eddie's house when I'd driven by yesterday and the day before.

What were they looking for?

Once inside the back door of The Laughing Loaf, I turned all lights on and set up a music playlist. I looked with pride at part of the special order Beck and I had worked on yesterday. We'd sculpted tiny fondant rats and softball bats for the cupcakes Mayor C would serve at today's River Grove River Rats practice. The cupcakes would be frosted in the team colors of blue and gold and adorned with the rats and bats. Beck and I managed to make the rats adorable.

When I checked the loaves in the proofer, my rye dough had risen and would be ready to bake this morning. I couldn't wait to taste the rich, earthy bread, punctuated by the bright, citrusy-anise flavor of caraway seeds.

At 6:30 a.m., Beck came in carrying her basket, full of eggs from her backyard chickens. Almost from the start, Beck had brought in eggs, and I realized pretty quickly that they tasted worlds better than what we could buy cheaply in quantity from the Costco in Santa Cruz. Against her protestations, I added an amount to her paycheck for the eggs we used. The brioche, kale tarragon frittata, and the Chief's egg on toast wouldn't be the same without them.

I looked up from slathering filling on the cinnamon roll dough to see what mood Beck was in. Normally a cheerful person, Beck's face showed exactly what she was thinking. Today, she looked thoughtful. Not worried, sad, or upset. Just thoughtful. Which made me curious.

"'Morning, Beck. How's it going?"

It took a while for her to answer.

"Okay, I guess," she said distractedly. Then she looked me in the eye. "So Brad was on a stakeout with the Chief at Eddie's house last night."

I nodded. "I passed them in Brad's truck this morning on my way in. Hear anything about how it went?"

She set the basket down on the counter and began filling the egg rack in the fridge. "Brad called Sam because he was bored last night. He said the lights were never on at the house. But he and the Chief both knew someone was in the house."

"Really? How did they know?" I waited for the rest.

"They saw someone bump the blinds and look out. When they got out, they heard a sliding door. So they went around the back of the house. Brad saw somebody running away, cutting through neighbors' yards. He tried to catch up with them, but the person disappeared."

I felt a prickle on the back of my neck. In my dream, Eddie had been alive. Was the picky Eddie Sumner haunting his own house from the grave, angry that people were "messing with his stuff"?

"I had a dream last night that Eddie was still alive. He was in his house yelling at people for getting into his things."

Beck's eyes grew wide. "That's scary. I mean, he's for sure dead, right?"

"He's dead all right. I was there when the medical examiner said it." I made up my mind to chat with the Chief if he came in today. "But I wonder if there's something in Eddie's house that somebody really wants. I can't figure out how they're getting inside."

Once we opened the doors, our weekend customers began coming in—a different crowd that twe saw on weekdays: parents with children in strollers, couples with their dogs, and a few people with board games gathering leisurely at the tables. In comparison to our weekday mornings, it was quiet and slow paced.

An adorable toddler wearing a Disney Princess costume came in with her dad, and I made sure she got a juice box and some Laughing Loaf Bakery stickers I'd had printed up —featuring Biga and a loaf of bread.

She gave me a look of delight and immediately peeled them all off and applied them to her face.

I WASN'T sure the Chief would come in today, but at 10 a.m. he and his granddaughter Chloe came in together. The results of the stakeout could be read on the Chief's face. There were dark shadows under his eyes. He looked exhausted and discouraged. Chloe on the other hand was in a chatty mood as they came up to order. She had her laptop bag slung over her shoulder.

"Gracie! Please tell me you have toaster pastries. They are the best things ever. I *must* have a toaster pastry." She stepped over to the display case to look at the options.

I laughed at her. "You're lucky. They're on the menu now."

"Chocolate hazelnut? I'll take that. And a matcha latte, please."

The Chief stepped up to order. "The usual for me— drip coffee with some cream. And egg on toast if you can make it."

"I can do that for you in just a few minutes. We've got fresh eggs this morning. Got any time to chat?" I asked. "At the corner table?"

He shrugged. "Why not. Come on over when you get a chance."

Fifteen minutes later, the line at the counter was gone, so I headed for the Chief and Chloe's table with his fried egg on whole wheat toast. Then I saw that Chloe had moved over to another table where two of her friends had settled and was laughing and speaking in low tones—which was probably for the best.

"Here you go, Dave." I laid the plate in front of him with a napkin and silverware. If you were used to having Beck's decadent chocolate beignets for breakfast, an egg on toast wasn't going to spark much joy. But the bread was fresh, and the egg was way better than anything you'd get at a diner.

"I sure do appreciate it, Gracie." The Chief nodded his thanks then sliced into the egg on toast and took a bite. "This is just what I needed after last night. Stakeouts are a young man's game. Brad and I traded off, but I didn't get much sleep in his truck."

"Any sign of the intruder?" I went up to grab my coffee from the counter and took Chloe's vacated seat. I'd heard this via Beck this morning, but I wanted to hear the Chief's version.

The Chief wolfed down half of his breakfast, washed it down with coffee then responded.

"No lights that we could see. We saw some movement in the house–someone bumped the blinds in the living room. So we got out and approached the house. We were approaching from the side of the house when we heard a door slam shut."

"What did you do?"

"Brad's faster than I am, so he took off into the back-yard. I saw someone running in the dark heading past that kid's playhouse into a neighbor's yard. The guy was in dark clothes - slim, a little on the short side–somewhere under five and a half feet." The Chief pushed a piece of toast around his plate till it was covered with egg yolk. "Brad was getting close, then the guy cut through another yard—one of the lots facing Pilgrim Way. Then he disappeared."

Great. The guy had headed for *my* street.

"I had a dream last night that Eddie was alive—he was the one in his house. Telling people to stay away from his stuff."

The Chief nodded. "Yeah, both Laura Freitas and the cleaner, Carleen, told us he could be that way. Kinda makes you wonder what he was keeping in his house."

"Can't you and Brad go through the house and search for whatever he might have had there?"

The Chief shrugged. "How would we know what to look for? Whoever's been in the house probably knows–and they can't find it."

I couldn't stop picking apart the situation. I had questions, and I'd sit there as long as the Chief would let me, trying to figure out who had been in Eddie Sumner's house.

"You say there was no sign of a break-in," I said, thinking this through. "And both women had keys to the house—which you say they turned in to you. But that doesn't mean anything. Even if they turned them in to you, they could have made copies."

"Miss Freitas told us she was in the process of ending her relationship with Mr. Sumner," the Chief said, looking wistfully at someone carrying a plateful of beignets past the table. "She told us she was about to give his key back to him and say goodbye—then she heard he'd been killed."

"I saw her in front of Eddie's house Thursday. She was on her way to talk to you and Brad. She didn't sound that sad about his death. Her biggest concern was that I was sticking my nose into her business."

The Chief chuckled and wore the biggest smile he had

all week. "C'mon, you gotta know you do that. You're a snoop, Gracie."

"Gee, thanks." I gave him a scowl. "With Eddie dead, we have to take her word for it that she was breaking up with him. She could have been out for revenge. Maybe he cheated on her. Maybe he treated her badly–which wouldn't surprise me. I mean, he did come into the bakery the day before Valentine's Day, looking for something to 'satisfy his obligation' to her."

The Chief pressed his lips together. "If he was a bad boyfriend, she could have gotten angry at him and let him have it with the first thing she got her hands on—the paperweight."

I finished the last of my latte.

"What do you know about Carleen Fuller?" I asked. "Mary Jo says she's a tough lady and that Eddie didn't bother her, since she's cleaned house for some pretty crazy people. Eddie paid her well, and she seemed to have no problems with him."

The Chief frowned, leaning his tired head on his hand. "Carleen's been struggling financially for years. Barely making ends meet. Eddie's well-off by River Grove standards. My fear is that she found out Eddie had something valuable in his house and she couldn't resist the temptation to take it. She did that once years ago—stole a piece of jewelry from a couple up on Oceanview, though she gave it right back when they confronted her. Maybe Eddie caught her in the act."

The Chief seemed to have thought this through. Was he just speculating based on her past, or had he picked up something from questioning her?

"Dave, what makes you think that?"

"She seemed to know a lot about Eddie's house. What

he kept where. She's someone who's done whatever she could to survive." The Chief shifted in his seat and shot a glance at his granddaughter, who was headed our way. "And it hasn't always been above board."

I wondered how long ago Carleen had stolen the jewelry. I was learning that River Grovians had a long memory when it came to their neighbors' misdeeds. People were defined by what they'd done twenty, thirty years ago.

I wanted to talk to Carleen. I wondered if Mary Jo could connect us.

The Chief had finished his food, and he slumped down in his chair.

"Gracie, I know you're good friends with Elana, but I've got to be up front with you. Kirk Schiffer is still our main person of interest," the Chief said. "He's withheld information from us. And he won't account for where he was during late afternoon when Eddie Sumner was killed. He's put us off for a few days now, saying he's finishing up some big product launch. But I'm going to have to take steps soon." He shook his head and tightened his lips.

"I can't drag him in to question him. But Brad and I will be looking for any evidence we can find. And as soon as we find it, there's going to be a warrant for Kirk Schiffer's arrest."

Chapter Eleven

That night, before I closed up at the bakery, I plopped down in the executive chair in my little closet office and ate a slice of the rye bread I'd baked today.

Eddie Sumner's murder was taking up way more brain space than I'd intended.

And now I was worried that my best friend's husband would be facing arrest soon.

Originally, I was worried about Sky, and I wanted him to be okay. Leanne Robbins had left me a message today thanking me for getting him help. Apparently, he'd met with Seth Gordon Friday evening. After talking through his experience, he was slowly returning to his extroverted self. She was pretty sure he'd be back at school on Monday.

But Eddie Sumner's death was another matter. When I worked in the tech industry back in Seattle, I specialized in solving problems. Eddie's death was an intriguing puzzle to me, without an obvious answer.

Obviously, Eddie was dead—but who was in his house?

And how had they gotten past the lock and deadbolt? What were they moving around in the house, night after night?

Then there was the matter of Kirk Schiffer. Eddie had been horrible to work with—and was responsible for the costly delay of BlueSurf's new Tsunami product launch. Kirk had a right to be angry. But hopefully, that frustration hadn't led him to murder his lead programmer.

Tonight I'd head home and try to catch Mary Jo before she and my dad left for the play.

My brain was a little too obsessed with this puzzle.

I wanted to ask Carleen Fuller some questions.

WHEN I CAME through the door, Biga snubbed me, which he sometimes did when he hadn't gone with me to the bakery. He went over to my father, who was wearing a fancy, somewhat dated black suit with a crisp white shirt. Mary Jo was dressed in a chunky silver necklace and a red dress that looked beautiful but must have dated back at least forty years. They looked well matched and a little like time travelers.

"You both look great," I said, genuinely. "Hope you enjoy the play."

"Mary Jo knows the director from back in the day," my father said, looking over at Mary Jo admiringly. "Forty years ago, she played Hero in his production of *Much Ado About Nothing*."

I was still getting used to seeing Mary Jo as this former actress—and not just someone who obsessed over actors and actresses in the tabloids.

"Mary Jo–if you've got time before you leave, I wanted to ask you a question."

Mary Jo, turned to me, her blingy necklace sparkling in the living room lights. She smiled warmly.

"Of course, Gracie."

"I talked to the Chief today about Eddie Sumner's murder. I'd really like to talk to your friend, Carleen, if I could. Could you tell her I'd like to speak with her?"

The kind, friendly smile on Mary Jo's face faded, replaced by a stern, set look. Her bubbly gracious demeanor was gone.

"I don't feel comfortable giving you Carleen's information, Gracie." Her tone was firm and she almost spat out the words. "I'll tell her you're interested in speaking with her, but it's up to her. She's been burned in the past. People in River Grove still spread rumors about her, even though they don't know anything about what her life has been like. If you do talk to her, show her some respect. She's not just a tool for you to use to solve another one of your cases. She's a human being."

My father was dumbfounded by this. He turned from me to Mary Jo—inspecting her as if somebody had slipped into the room and taken the place of the woman he was attending the theatre with.

I hadn't expected this response, since Mary Jo had been bending over backwards to be nice to me for months.

After they left, I sank down onto the couch and let out a long sigh. I wasn't insulted, just puzzled.

I was seeing a very different side of my father's girlfriend.

Nate arrived about a half an hour after my dad and Mary Jo left, after I'd finished preparing dinner for him and me. I saw him approach, but it seemed like it took forever for him to get to the door. He also hadn't ridden his bike like he usually did. His Honda was parked in front of the house.

When I opened the door, he slowly lifted one leg then the other to step into the house, walking like Frankenstein.

Nate was one of the most stoic people I knew. He bore up under pain or injury with an almost superhuman strength. He told me he'd once dragged himself back from a hike with a broken leg. So to see him have difficulty walking up my front steps with his lips pressed together, at the pace of a 90-year-old grandma, showed me this injury was bad.

"How bad was practice?"

Nate grimaced and his eyes shifted away from me. "Looks like I pulled an adductor muscle when I jumped to catch Councilman Gregg's pop fly."

"Did you catch it?"

"Of course." He smirked. I gave him a high five.

"So what's an *adductor* muscle?" I took out my phone and immediately Googled it. Then I found it. To my dismay, the article was very specific. And had very detailed illustrations, in color. *Yikes.*

"So—you have a pulled groin."

My boyfriend turned red. "It's a lot more embarrassing when you say it that way, Gracie."

Our romantic evening was definitely off the table.

"You might as well get comfortable," I said with a quiet sigh. Judging from what I'd just read, he must be in a lot of pain. "Tell me what would help. What's more comfortable? Lying down, standing or sitting?"

He groaned again. "It hurt bad sitting down in the car to drive here. So maybe lying down. I could use some ice if you have any. And ibuprofen?"

I led him to the sofa. He winced as he gingerly lowered himself to sit then stretched out his long legs on the sofa. Meanwhile, I got a bag of frozen peas out of the freezer. I let him place it where it was most comfortable, since—uh—that wasn't really my job here. I handed him two ibuprofen and some water.

I laid an oversized pillow up against the sofa and leaned my back against it. He bent down and kissed the top of my head.

"Maybe my idea for a make-up session tonight was too optimistic," he said weakly. "I should have called this off and stayed home."

I leaned back and smiled at him. "If it's a choice between you lying on your sofa at home and lying on my sofa, I'm glad you're here."

He gave me a weary look. "I'm *so* glad I'm on your sofa."

I craned my neck around to see him. "I made salmon and risotto. I just have to warm it up."

"I'm starving. I also want to hear about your day. You're probably more up to date about the Eddie Sumner case than I am."

I went to plate up dinner and pour us glasses of wine. From the living room, I heard him call.

"By the way, I loved the treats you made for us. Rats and bats. I couldn't stop laughing when I saw the cupcakes, Gracie. I can't believe Mayor C didn't think they were funny."

With some effort, Nate turned himself onto his side so he could eat.

As we ate, I told him about my conversation with the Chief—about Laura Freitas's defensiveness and his suspicions about Carleen Fuller, based on her past. And how he still considered Kirk Schiffer the chief suspect.

"Elana's hearing the gossip about Kirk, and she's upset. But I don't think she knows how seriously the Chief suspects him. I told her she needs to encourage Kirk to make himself available for questioning." I stacked our empty plates on the coffee table. "I don't understand why he's not doing that."

Nate lay on his side, still looking in pain. His light blue eyes looked thoughtful—and very dreamy.

"I wonder if Kirk is so angry with what Eddie did to his product launch that he doesn't want to lift a finger to bring justice for him. You said you've never seen him like this."

"Yeah, it's just weird. He's not acting like the Kirk I know."

"If Kirk killed Eddie, I think he'd be acting differently. He'd be more worried about his image, what the Chief thought of him. But Kirk told me once that he funded his startup personally. He's built that company from the ground up. Kirk is so mad at what Eddie put his startup through that he's completely shut down."

"But logically that doesn't make sense." I frowned, leaning back against Nate's arm. "He's only hurting himself —and Elana."

"I didn't say what he's doing makes sense. But I do know something about anger. It's like a gun that fires backwards. Even if you aim it at someone else, you end up hitting yourself first."

Nate could be right; in the past month, I'd seen the anger in Kirk's eyes. Eddie Sumner had pushed him to the limit.

Nate had an insight into how people think, and he'd come about it the hard way, by dealing with a lot of pain, loss, and anger himself.

I sat up and bent over him to give him a long slow kiss on the lips, which he returned.

Because tonight, that part of him was the only part that didn't hurt.

When Nate fell asleep on the sofa, I got out a comforter for him. I covered him and let him sleep.

Biga jumped up on the sofa and settled himself into the space next to Nate's feet.

I grabbed my pillow and blanket and curled up in my father's recliner for the night.

When my father got home around 11 p.m., I heard him say a congenial good night to both of us as if this was something we did every night.

Chapter Twelve

At 4:30 a.m., I woke up, went through my morning routine, then loaded up the coffeemaker in the kitchen and left a few scones wrapped for Nate.

Getting Biga into the crate was hard. He didn't want to give up his comfy spot next to Nate. When Biga realized I was serious about leaving, he finally jumped off the sofa and crawled into the crate.

I drove down Sunnyside since I'd gotten into the habit this week. There were no lights on at Eddie's. I didn't see any cars on that stretch of the street. Brad's truck wasn't on the street doing surveillance. It was cold this morning, and there was a bite in the air.

Beck came through the back door of the bakery at 6:30 a.m., pink-cheeked from the cold and eager to bake.

"Can I put on the Irish pop? I'm so into it now. I can't get the songs out of my head."

"Go ahead, Beck." Beck was obsessed by a soft pop song by the Irish band, The Blizzards. She knew all the words. So we heard the song a *lot*.

"I've got three batches of cinnamon roll dough ready to

fill and roll up. After that, I can fill the frittata shells for you so you can get the beignets going."

"Thanks, Gracie. I think people are going to want warm things this morning."

"And the dining area will be packed."

Before we opened, when I had a moment's break, I picked up my phone and texted Elana to see if she'd be up for meeting at The Riverside tonight. Nate's words last night had stuck with me. I had more sympathy for Kirk, yet I also knew his time was running out. He had to meet with the Chief.

During our mid-morning lull, I checked my phone to find two messages.

> Thanks for the coffee and scones. 🩶🩶🩶

> Had good breakfast chat with your dad.
> Drove myself home at 8:30 and survived.
> Drs appt at 10 😬

Then Elana's response to my text:

> The Riverside. Yes, please! I need a break
> from K so bad. Pick me up at 7?

THAT EVENING, Elana and I took our seats at a candlelit table, with a glimpse of the San Luciano River through the trees, in The Riverside Saloon's dining area. The place wasn't crowded.

Since it was a Sunday night, there were no headlining bands performing, only an acoustic guitarist and standup bass playing a low-key set of jazz covers on the stage to the side of the room. It was a nice change from the full-on, high decibel concerts that tended to be playing whenever Elana and I came to the Riverside. I breathed a sigh of relief: we'd actually be able to hear each other.

"I can't tell you how good it feels to be here, Gracie." Elana was already sounding brighter and more like her lively self. "When Kirk isn't at BlueSurf, he's home moping around. He haunts the house like an angry, depressed ghost. I kicked him out yesterday and told him to go for a hike."

"How are things going at BlueSurf?" Kirk was probably dealing with the aftermath of Eddie's loss.

"They're moving out of chaos mode," Elana said, looking eagerly at the waiter coming back to our table. "They had to bring on a few more programmers, just to tie up the loose ends Eddie left behind. And those were the loose ends he left behind *before* he was killed."

As the waiter reached our table, I realized it was Manny, a musician who played keyboard in a local band that performed occasionally at The Riverside. He handed us menus.

Elana asked Manny to bring her a cosmopolitan. I smiled at the waiter.

"And I'll have a gin and tonic."

Elana sighed and sat back in her chair. "I don't feel like I know Kirk anymore, Gracie. This isn't the guy I married. He's angry. He's bitter about what happened."

I told her Nate's theory, about why he thought Kirk couldn't bring himself to talk to the police about Eddie.

"Nate could be right." Elana sniffled just a bit. "I mean, it doesn't take more than a few minutes of conversation to see that he's still mad at Eddie. It's his company, and he's taking it very personally. That makes it look like Kirk had a reason to kill him."

"The Chief is ready to go to BlueSurf to meet with him." It wasn't something she wanted to hear.

Elana started to sniff again, and I handed her a tissue. "Gracie, please. Let's talk about something else. I can't do anything about this."

"I had an interesting interaction with Mary Jo Saturday night." I told her about Mary Jo's response when I asked her if she could introduce me to Carleen.

"So she stood up for her friend," Elana said, still blotting her eyes. "That's a good thing."

"She's been trying a little too hard to win my approval. And this—defending Carleen—was really important to her. She was willing to risk losing my approval to protect her friend. That made me like her more."

Elana could be a bit scattered, but she looked like she was really listening to me now. A few months ago, she and I had a falling out, here at the Riverside. We were still working our way back from that, but it was going well.

"You said Mary Jo is really different from your mom." She looked curious "What was your mom like? You told me she died when you were young." She looked at me and lowered her voice to a whisper. "It's not going against your witness protection rules for you to tell me, is it?"

Because I was in witness protection, there had been so many things I couldn't say for so long. So many weird lies I'd told, pre-written backstories I had to stick to, since I'd gone into WITSEC.

But the idea of my mom being a federally protected secret made me laugh.

"She was quiet, very proper. She had a great sense of humor. She loved music and every day she spent an hour playing the grand piano in the living room. It was like she was in another world when she played. She was a very wise woman. Sometimes I feel that if she hadn't died when she did, I wouldn't have married my ex. She would have warned me it was a bad idea."

Elana leaned on her hand as she listened to me, a half-smile on her face. "Yeah, but you might have done it anyway, Gracie."

"Maybe." I smirked. "Anyway, I'm moving on from the past. I am trying to live in the moment because it's actually really good. My new employee at the bakery, Maeve, is great. She, Beck, and I work well together. And things with Nate are...so good. Though he hurt himself at the River Rats practice yesterday." I told her about Nate's injury, on the night he'd been planning a quiet romantic evening for the two of us. "And last night was a makeup session for our Valentine's date last week, when I fell asleep on him."

Elana, who had just taken a sip of her cosmo, almost did a spit take. She started laughing into her napkin. Then I started laughing, watching her laugh.

"Gracie, I can't believe you two." This time when she blotted her eyes it was because she'd been laughing so hard. "Poor Nate. I'm sorry to laugh, but Mayor C works that team to death. Kirk was on the River Rats two years ago, and he said it almost finished him off."

"Nate had a telehealth appointment with an ER doctor today. He'll be out of action for a month." Nate told me he'd have to reschedule a couple of photo shoots. He couldn't do the hiking required to get to the birds.

When Manny came by again, we ordered dinner. Typical of Elana's and my nights out, it was a table full of appetizers and charcuterie, and lots of red wine.

After the acoustic duo took a break, Reggie McFerrin himself—seventy-something, former hippie and owner of the Riverside—stopped by to talk to us. He wore a black three-piece-suit and a purple tie, and of course, his standard sunglasses, even inside. In the time I'd known him, he'd gone from being someone I feared a little bit, to being a trusted friend, even an advisor.

"Good to see you ladies here tonight. I'm sorry this isn't dancing music, Elana."

Elana smiled sadly. "Thanks, but I'm not in a dancing mood tonight, Reggie."

"I understand." Reggie bowed and pressed his hands together in a *namaste* gesture, his way of showing support. "I'm thinking of you and Kirk. Enjoy your dinner, and I will be hoping for the best for you both."

In the next twenty minutes, Elana and I devoured way too many appetizers, downed all our wine, and one more time laughed so hard we almost cried. One thing we had in common was the complete lack of an off switch when it came to eating and drinking. I'd probably pay for it when I tried to get out of bed in the morning, but Elana's improved mood was worth it.

Before I dropped her off at her house, she gave me a hug.

"Thank you, Gracie. This is what I needed." She looked like she was going to cry again.

"I can deal with all of this for one more day now. I just hope Eddie's killer is found soon."

Chapter Thirteen

My late evening of food and drink hit me like a brick to the head the next day.

I sluggishly pulled myself out of bed and showered, which woke me up somewhat. I resorted to a cup of coffee from the drip coffeemaker, which to me didn't really qualify as coffee, in comparison to what Beck made on the expensive Italian espresso machine at the bakery.

I came up with a new term for it: *pre-coffee.*

It was the brown liquid I drank in order to get me to a place where I could get real coffee.

Beck was a little too much of her cheery self for me this morning. When she squealed with delight at seeing Maeve returning from her soiree and weekend in Napa, it hit my aching head like a sledgehammer.

Maeve wanted to talk about the party she'd helped with at Le Pain Parisienne on Friday. As she turned on the industrial mixer to start the brioche dough, it sent another wave of pain through my head. Then she proceeded to talk loudly over the mixer, describing the pastries and bread she'd worked on.

I went to my office and downed two ibuprofen with a big swig from my water bottle.

"Maeve, let's talk about rye when you get a chance. I made two different batches this weekend. I'd like to do a taste test and have you work on a larger batch this week. We'll intro the rye loaves at the beginning of March."

"That sounds brilliant, Gracie." Maeve said, switching off the mixer. "I'm a rye fan and I can never find loaves I like."

After things calmed down in town—and hopefully after Eddie's killer was found—I'd talk to Beck and Maeve about my idea of introducing a lunch menu with sandwiches. The more I thought about it, the more excited I got about launching it this year.

THE HIGH SCHOOLERS flooded in at 7 a.m.

I saw Sky walk in with Dakota and Jeb, messenger bag over his shoulder. He looked like his old self. Beck grinned at me from the espresso machine.

Once he got in line, he was swamped by young women expressing their sympathy. And by the look on Sky's face, he was really enjoying it.

"Welcome back, Sky," I said when he came up to the counter. "We missed you. I had nobody to groan at my jokes."

"You need that accountability, Ms. Markley." He lowered his voice as I set his cappuccino and cinnamon roll on the counter. "Hey, my mom said you got the Chief to let me talk to Seth. Thanks."

"Glad it worked out." I flashed a smile at him, and then he was pulled away by two young women who wanted to hear his story. Dakota frowned. She moved to sit with friends at another table.

I heard Sky's voice as he explained to the two young women. "I'm afraid I can't tell you *everything*. Legal restrictions, you know."

When Maeve came to work, she overflowed with stories of her bakes for the weekend, and the event she'd help cater for Le Pain Parisienne. I showed her the rye loaves I'd baked, and we tasted the bread with different toppings including a mini-Reuben with sauerkraut, Swiss cheese, and pastrami. Maeve may not have had as much official experience with breadmaking, but she'd worked at one of the most famous bakeries in the country: Night Rose in Sonoma. I valued her opinions.

For the past few months, I'd been toying with the idea of offering lunch at The Laughing Loaf, with sandwich offerings. While Beck continued to add to our pastry menu, I wanted to expand our bread selection. We could provide more take-home bread options and a lunch menu for takeout and in-house dining.

Around lunchtime, Carleen Fuller called me and left a message.

I listened in my office. Since most people texted me, I had to figure out where voice mail messages were stored on my phone.

"Gracie, this is Carleen Fuller." The woman's voice was weak and hoarse, sounding like a much older woman than I'd pictured. She had traces of a Texas accent. "My friend Mary Jo told me you wanted to talk to me about my time housecleaning for Eddie Sumner. Give me a call back and we can set up a time."

I called her right back, and she answered in a shaky voice.

"Carleen, this is Gracie. Can we meet tonight? I can come to you. Just let me know."

Carleen hesitated.

"I live in a room at River Grove Trailer Park. I'm staying with a family there. I'm kinda an on-call grandma to their kids. It's gonna be a little crowded, but we can talk outside if we need to." She gave me her address. "I'll see you at 5 p.m."

All day, I thought about my talk with Carleen. The fact that she'd called me back pretty quickly made me wonder if she wasn't just being helpful; she had a reason for wanting to talk to me. I had to be realistic. Maybe the Chief's instinct was right. She'd stolen before on her house-cleaning gig; maybe she'd done it again. If she'd killed Eddie because she'd been caught stealing his precious "stuff," this could be a way to put out her version of the story.

I was more likely to be sympathetic to her than the Chief would be.

I dropped Biga off with my dad after Beck, and I closed up at The Laughing Loaf.

My little dog was happy to be out of his crate and did not look back. He had no further need of me.

So I gave my dad a hug, got in my car, and set out for River Grove Trailer Park.

The sun had dipped behind the trees as I drove west, following the curves of the highway. River Grove Trailer Park was about a mile outside of River Grove. Aiden Franzi, who sometimes helped out at the bakery with his friend Chloe Westerman, lived here with his mother.

Light was fading as I pulled off the highway and turned onto a short access road that led into the trailer park loop, nestled in a large clearing surrounded by redwoods. It looked a little like a campground. Kids played on swings in a small playground area.

I followed the loop to #22—a white double-wide that needed some sprucing up. Some of the window screens hung in tatters. As I pulled up in one of the dirt parking spots near the trailer, I heard a baby crying through an open window. A young woman sounded like she was lecturing her kids in Spanish.

I knocked on the door and waited, looking at the rusted mailbox and hanging wires where there used to be a doorbell.

A small wiry woman with a tanned face and a thin grey ponytail opened the door. She nodded outside.

"Hi there, Gracie. Marisol and her kids are getting ready for dinner. It's crazy in here. Why don't we sit outside on one of the picnic tables?"

The wind whipping through the trailer park was chilling, so I zipped up my hoodie. We sat at a table near the playground, where kids chased each other and screamed, in that last burst of activity before they would go inside for dinner.

"Mary Jo said you solve murders." She looked me up and down, as if trying to figure out if that was something I was cut out for.

"I've helped with a few around town." I nodded. "In Eddie's case, one of my delivery helpers found his body, so I got involved that way. Mary Jo told me you did house-cleaning for him once a week."

"For the past two years." Carleen leaned her bony, sun-spotted arms on the table and raised her eyebrows. "He was sure persnickety. There were rooms in the house I couldn't go into. I wasn't allowed to look in some closets and his desk.

But he paid me a lot of money. Money I wouldn't be able to make anywhere else. Probably to keep me quiet."

"What do you mean, to keep you *quiet?*" A crackle of electricity surged through me. So Eddie was hiding something in his house.

"When he was working at home, Eddie would get boxes delivered by a guy in a white van. He'd put them in the rooms that were off-limits to me. A few times when I was there later in the day, he'd bring paper bags out and hand them off to people who came to the door. They paid him cash."

Maybe Eddie was a drug dealer. Maybe he was dealing in black market prescription drugs. Or at the least involved in some kind of multilevel marketing scheme. I wondered if this had been Eddie's real moneymaking job. Maybe the work he'd done with this scheme cut into his time with BlueSurf, causing him to slip on his programming deadlines —and delay BlueSurf's big release date.

"What about the girlfriend—Laura?" I asked. "Was she involved in this?"

Carleen tilted her head and thought about it. "Laura was at the house most of the time. But I never saw her going into the rooms to get the stuff. She never talked to the people coming to the door. She was usually working on her computer in the living room."

I lay my hands on the picnic table. "Carleen, were you ever tempted to look in the rooms? Figure out what was in the boxes? I'd be going crazy, wanting to know."

A dark look came over Carleen's face. "I'm sure the Chief told you. Twenty years ago, I was in a bad place. I was drinking—not sober like I am now. So I took something from a woman's house I was cleaning. An expensive diamond ring. I never saw her wear it, so I didn't think she'd miss it. She went to the police and told them I'd stolen it."

She shrugged and the corners of her mouth turned up. "Sure, I stole it. I'm not saying that was a smart thing to do, but I couldn't pay my rent. I returned it the next day, but nobody's ever forgotten about it. Now I go into a house to clean, and I keep my head down. I do my job. I don't take nothing, and I don't ask questions."

I could see why she wouldn't want to ruin a good thing. Eddie paid her well.

"You don't have to worry about Eddie now. He's dead."

"I told Chief Westerman when he asked me in for questioning." Carleen's lips pressed together tightly. "I told him I thought Eddie was running some kind of illegal operation from his house. I told him about the locked rooms. He moved on to the next question."

"But if the stuff—whatever Eddie was receiving and selling—is still there... I mean, there's the proof." Had the Chief and Brad searched the house? Then the thought hit me: with the intruder's visits, the shipments could be long gone.

Carleen looked at me as if she and I were living in completely different worlds.

"Why would they listen to me? What if they end up accusing me of his murder? Maybe they'd say I tried to take Eddie's stuff—and when he caught me, I killed him."

I wanted to tell her that I'd talk to the Chief on her behalf, and that I'd help make things right. But there was no way I could guarantee that.

Her experience was telling her that would make things worse.

I wondered if Mary Jo, when considering whether to connect me with Carleen, had come to the same conclusion.

Chapter Fourteen

The high schoolers came in early Tuesday morning wearing a rainbow of hair styles and colors, as part of RGHS Spirit Week.

River Grove High's basketball team was playing a rival high school on the coast Friday, so every day this week featured some activity to build team spirit.

Today was Crazy Hair Day.

I looked out from the counter to see a room of mohawks, multicolored sprayed hair, pink wigs, Princess Leia cinnamon bun hair, and pigtails that defied gravity. Not everyone participated in the week's activities. Anyone involved in sports or student government had done their hair, while anyone outside of those groups either did something simple or didn't participate at all.

Jeb looked completely normal. He ordered at the counter then took his drink to a table and began doing homework. Chloe Westerman already had her purple underlayer of hair. She had just pulled it up in a messy bun to show off her color. Again, wordlessly, she took a seat at the table, across from Jeb, and began doing homework. At some point, I'd ask her what was going on; within a week she seemed to have changed her attitude to Jeb. The curiosity was killing me.

After most people were seated, Sky Robbins came in and joined the line, wearing what looked like a beehive wig, painted white and silver. There was something stuck to the top of it. Everyone at the tables was watching him and pointing. When he got to the counter, I asked him.

"So, what's this new look, Sky?"

He looked at me as if should be obvious. "I'm the iceberg, Ms. Markley. And this—" he tapped a small boat near the top of the beehive "—is the Titanic."

I started laughing. Beck turned around from the espresso machine and cracked up. Maeve heard the laughter, and came out from the back room and took a picture with her phone.

"You're brilliant, Sky," Maeve said excitedly. "If there's a contest at school today, I hope you win."

Sky bowed his icy head to her, and it looked like he blushed a little.

When the Chief and Mayor C came in for coffee and breakfast, I told the Chief I needed to talk to him. I wanted to tell him what I'd heard from Carleen.

He raised his eyebrows and invited me to pull up a chair at their table. "Tell me what's going on, Gracie." He glanced over at Mayor C, whose eyes were wide with interest at anything I might share about the case.

"I spent some time with Carleen Fuller yesterday. She thinks Eddie was running some kind of illegal operation at his house. He received shipments and then people would pick up deliveries." I told him how Carleen wasn't allowed to go into two of the rooms or touch certain things on Eddie's desk.

The Chief looked skeptical, maybe because the source of information was Carleen.

"She didn't tell me that when I questioned her last week." The Chief frowned. I wanted to tell him: *Maybe she didn''t think you would believe her.*

"Dave, did you and Brad do a search of the house?" Mayor C turned to the Chief.

"We searched the scene of the crime—the garage. Then we went in the house to make sure there were no assailants inside."

"But did you check all the rooms?" I asked.

"We saw some moving boxes which looked innocent enough. We weren't looking for illegal goods. It was a murder scene." The Chief sounded defensive. He grunted and poked the yolk of his egg with his fork. "Brad and I will do a search this morning."

"Our intruder's had a few days. He—or she—may have cleared the rooms out by now," I said. Any contraband, whatever it was, could be gone.

"Chief, I have a theory that our intruder had a set of keys made last week—for the front, garage and sliding doors. From keys they got from somebody in Eddie's house."

The Chief looked distracted, as he texted someone. Hopefully it was Brad about searching Eddie's house. "Have you talked to the Schulz brothers at Key Haus, Gracie? They're just down the street."

I made a note to walk down to the small key store when I had a chance.

As I headed back to the counter, Mayor C stood up and approached me, her voice quiet. "Nate told me he's out of commission for a month. The doctor said no practices." She looked upset. "I didn't realize how bad his injury was. Can you tell him I'm sorry? I'm starting to think I put a little too much pressure on the team."

"Corinne, why don't you tell him yourself?" My head still pounded, and I was really trying to be patient. "I think he'd appreciate that."

At 12:15 p.m., I looked out the window of the back room at the clear, brisk day and I decided I'd take Biga for a walk. I had a few too many things in my head, and I needed a break.

I left Beck and Maeve busy on tarts and bread, respectively. They had the music going and were cheerfully singing and conversing as they did their duties in the back room, in between going out front to serve customers. Beck had tutored Maeve in the workings of our espresso machine, so Maeve was able to step up to barista duties when needed.

I snapped Biga's leash on, and Biga excitedly pulled me toward the door. We stepped out into the cool, sunny day and I immediately felt better.

We walked down toward The Riverside, then cut through to the river trail. A light wind rustled through the branches of the redwoods. I took in a deep breath as Biga stopped excitedly to sniff and water every bush on the trail where other dogs had left their mark.

I've always wondered what goes through a dog's head as he checks out the clues left by other dogs.

Sparky from over on Conifer Street was here
Doodlebug, visiting from Santa Cruz, says hi
Yo, it's Pete, a German Shepherd from up on Charley Road.
Stay cool, guys!

I looked up at the back side of The Riverside Saloon. No sign of Reggie McFerrin, who liked to come out on the balcony to take in his view of the river. When Elana and I had fled the Russian spies back in October, we'd gotten to see Reggie's office and the spacious balcony, certainly one of the best views in River Grove.

A couple of moms piloting strollers with sleepy toddlers inside passed me and said hi. I recognized them from their visits to the bakery during the day.

Biga and I walked on toward the redwood grove. We were almost there, when I saw a figure in the trees ahead of us, partially hidden by foliage. We were the only ones on this part of the trail, and my chest tightened.

Suddenly Biga strained on his leash, heading right for the figure.

"Biga, stop!"

He pulled hard, and I had no choice but to follow him as we headed into the dark of the clearing.

I came face to face with Kirk Schiffer.

His face looked grey and gaunt. He must have gone a few days without a shave. I shivered and hesitated at the edge of the clearing. I shouldn't be afraid. This was Kirk, who'd made brunch for me many times. Who was a good husband to my best friend. Who'd come to help when a killer smashed the front window of my bakery.

Elana hadn't been exaggerating. Kirk did look like an angry, depressed ghost. That didn't seem to bother Biga, who ran right up to Kirk and put his paws up on the man's leg. Kirk bent down to ruffle Biga's fur, and Biga began licking the man's hands.

"Gracie." Kirk nodded at me.

"How are things going, Kirk?"

"Not great." He shrugged. "I needed to get outside for a walk. Away from work. And home."

"Elana told me the product launch is finally coming together."

He grimaced. "After hiring a team of programmers to try to fix the mess Eddie made. I can't believe I put up with him for as long as I did. I hired him three years ago and I was so impressed by his experience that I didn't give him the oversight I should have. He used my startup. He strung us along. It's almost like he had another job, and we got his leftovers. He almost wrecked us." As Kirk spoke, the lines on his face grew deeper. I thought about Nate's comment, about Kirk's anger at Eddie shutting him down.

"When was the last time you saw Eddie? At BlueSurf?" I watched his face grow paler and I knew the answer. He paused then spoke, hoarsely.

"I saw him at his house. On Valentines Day. A little before 5 p.m. I went to see him because I was so angry."

This was right in the window of time in which Medical Examiner Martin Ito said Eddie was killed. I took a deep breath. I was standing next to a man who'd been angry enough to kill. And his alibi put him at the murder scene at the right time. I'd known Kirk for two years, yet fear gripped me. It must have been obvious by the look on my face.

"Gracie, I didn't do it. You know that, right? I didn't kill Eddie Sumner." He shook his head, torment in his eyes.

"Then you need to talk to the Chief." I tugged Biga's leash to signal that we were heading back. I gave him a curt nod. "Because he's looking for any reason he can find to arrest you."

Chapter Fifteen

The Laughing Loaf was quiet when I came in the back door. Maeve was shaping loaves, and I heard Beck's cheerful patter with customers over the sound of the espresso machine as she made coffee drinks up front.

"Gracie," Maeve looked over at me from the metal bread table with floured hands. "The Chief was here a few minutes ago looking for you."

"Did he say what he wanted?"

She shook her head. "He wanted to update you about something. He said you should go see him when you get a chance."

I couldn't desert my post again today, so I texted the Chief that I'd be over when we closed.

"Maeve, are you up for tasting some rye?" I'd been craving it all day. I had two loaves made from two different recipes. I wanted to decide which one to go with for next month's featured bread.

Her head popped up from the bread she was kneading. "Of course."

I cut up slices from the two loaves and arranged them on a bread board.

One recipe was based on a New York deli rye bread and included caraway seeds. The other included dark rye flour and sourdough starter for a tangier slice.

I liked both, but I needed another opinion. Though Maeve hadn't been allowed to bake at her former employer's, her time up north at the world-famous Night Rose bakery had given her a great palate for bread flavors.

Maeve took a cube of the deli rye and ate it. She nodded.

"That's really good."

She opened up her water bottle and took a gulp.

Then she popped a cube of sourdough rye into her mouth. She closed her eyes as she chewed.

"Hmmmm. I like the sourdough a little better, but just because it's more interesting to me. The deli rye is a great version of that bread, and I bet it will be more popular.

"Fair enough," I said with a smile. "That's what I was thinking."

I gave Maeve the deli rye recipe I'd written up so she could mix up a test batch this week.

I wrapped up the sourdough rye and set it aside in my office. I was stopping by Nate's tonight to keep him company, and he'd be all over any sourdough-rye combo.

After Beck and I closed up for the day, I loaded up my car with my things, including Biga's crate, and walked across the street with my dog to see the Chief. I noticed a car parked on the street near City Hall. Kirk Schiffer's Audi coupe. Had Kirk finally come to see the Chief?

I walked past Peony Roberts, city hall gatekeeper, who was engrossed in a phone call that sounded non-business related, judging by her flirtatious tone. Her eyes followed me as I walked past her, and she glared at me. She did not end her call to come after me.

Mayor C saw me go past her office and I heard her call out.

"Gracie!" She stood up and waved me in.

She lowered her voice. "Kirk Schiffer's in with the Chief."

Relief filled me. "Oh, my God. That's great!" I half-whispered it since we were two doors down from the Chief's office.

She nodded and kept her voice low. "Don't know what will come of it, but I sincerely hope Kirk had nothing to do with Eddie's death."

"Me, too." I sighed. "The Chief told me to come over after I closed up. Any idea of what he wanted to talk to me about?"

"He and Brad did their search of Eddie Sumner's house this morning. They didn't find anything. No drugs, no stolen goods of any kind. Looks like that was a dead end."

"They searched everything? Even that playhouse in the backyard?"

"The Chief said that was empty."

The intruder, whoever it was, had had several nights to clean the place out. I tried to imagine what Eddie could have been hiding in his house.

If we pinned down the identity of the intruder, I had a feeling we'd find a large quantity of Eddie's stuff.

Stuff the intruder definitely didn't want anyone to touch.

Back in my car with Biga, I texted Nate. After finding out Kirk had gone to see the Chief, I felt so much better.

Need company tonight?

Come eat with me, G. Mayor C's bringing me dinner.

Because apparently I can't cook without my groin.

So it's a guilt offering

Yep, but I'll take it. It's Mexican food. With flan!

Perfect!

See you at 6 🤍

I took Biga home and found Mary Jo in the kitchen roasting a chicken, while my dad was preparing a salad.

Meaning he had to open a package and dump it into a bowl.

After Mary Jo's weird comment about talking to Carleen on Saturday night, I didn't know what to say to her. But I greeted her and my dad with hugs and excused myself to feed Biga and take him out in the backyard for a runaround.

Then I called out goodbye to the chefs in the kitchen and darted out the door to drive to my boyfriend's house.

Nate greeted me at the door with a kiss.

"Look at you" I said, impressed. "You're up and around already."

He flashed a smile. "Still in pain. But I can't lie around all day. Besides I've spent enough time today sitting down at my computer doing finances and cleaning out all my photo files."

I took out the wrapped bread and set it on his kitchen

counter. "I brought you a loaf of rye bread, the sourdough version."

"I love rye." He picked it up and sniffed it. Then gave me another kiss. "Now I'm dreaming about sandwiches."

I smiled coyly, as I thought about my plans for The Laughing Loaf.

"Your dream just might come true—soon."

WE SAT down in his dining room and ate Mexican food while I told Nate all the latest news: meeting with Carleen Fuller and her suggestion that Eddie had been running some kind of illegal operation out of his home, but that Brad and the Chief's search of the house turned up nothing. I told him about my chance meetup with Kirk on my walk today, which hopefully got him to meet with the Chief and answer questions.

"I am relieved to hear about Kirk," Nate put his hand over mine.

"You were right about him. Kirk was completely shut down about Eddie, he was so angry. I was a little scared talking to him today. Turns out he *was* at Eddie's that day, yelling at him, at around 5 p.m.. And that's right around the time that the medical examiner said Eddie died."

Nate sat back in his chair, a frown on his face. He looked concerned.

"That's a little too close for comfort. The Chief couldn't arrest him, could he?"

"I don't think he has the evidence. That's what's been frustrating the Chief. He can't force Kirk to come in for questioning. And the only evidence is the fingerprints on the award."

Nate pushed the rest of his flan away. The look of intensity in his blue eyes melted me a little.

"Gracie, why is life in a small town so stressful?"

Both of us had come to River Grove from big cities—LA for him, Seattle for me. We were newcomers to small town life, still learning how it worked. Both of us were touched by the love and concern our new town had shown us. We'd made friends here quickly, and those friendships were strong and deep.

If Mayor C put the word out that Nate needed meals—which she probably would—he'd be set for the rest of his convalescence. When I'd injured my ribs back in December, my father and I were lavished on with meals and visits from well-wishers.

I moved over next to Nate and wrapped my hand around his.

"Even if it's a little crazy right now, I wouldn't want to be anywhere else."

He held my hand up to his face and kissed it.

"Me either."

We played a board game, a bird-based game called Wingspan, which—big surprise—Nate won. Then we cuddled for a bit and engaged in some light "snogging," as my Brit father would call it.

At 9 p.m., I headed home along the highway, crossing through downtown, then turning onto Sunnyside. I did this, probably because this route had become a habit this week.

I did hope some solution would miraculously appear at Eddie's house. Seeing the killer's name spelled out on his front lawn in river rocks would be helpful. Eddie's murder would be solved, and my friend's husband would be off the hook, innocent without question.

But the street was dead, as usual. No lights on at

Eddie's. Only porch lights on at a few houses on the street. I drove on and turned onto Pilgrim.

There was no orange bug parked on the street.

I parked in the carport and went inside.

"Welcome back, dear. How's Nate?" My father was back in his recliner with a snifter of brandy, watching a physics lecture on his iPad. He looked surprisingly content.

"Still in pain but doing a little better. It'll be a few more weeks till he's back to normal. Mayor C brought him a meal. Which I helped him eat."

My father snorted. "Mayor C owed him that."

"Where's Mary Jo? It's an early evening for you guys."

An emotion I couldn't identify crossed my father's face. He looked down at his iPad. "We decided we'd needed a break from each other for a few days. We'd been making dinner together most nights for the past few weeks."

I have to admit, my first thought was: *Thank God. I get my kitchen back.*

I scrutinized his face. "Did you both decide this?"

"It was my decision." My father looked at me across the tops of his wire-rimmed glasses. "We had been having a lot of fun, but it was starting to become—well, a bigger commitment than what I want right now."

I wondered how Mary Jo took the news.

"She thought I was breaking up with her. Which isn't true." My father looked a little sad as he said it. "I care about her a great deal. I want to spend time with friends, not only with her. I want to do more tutoring. You were right, Gracie. I want to do more of it. Working with the students makes me happier than almost anything right now."

"Good for you." Biga came into the room and jumped up into my lap. "You've really been thinking about this."

"Mary Jo and I are meeting next week at a steak house

to talk." He said, with a note of finality. "I want to continue to see her, but I'm not sure what her feelings are about this."

I smiled hopefully. I got up and gave him a kiss on the cheek. Biga trotted over with me. "Whichever way it goes, you will be okay, Dad. Things are opening up for you in this town. I think you'll be more than okay."

❦

I woke up at 3:30 the next morning, after having a dream about Eddie Sumner and his house.

In my dreams, there was a secret basement accessed through the garage, where Eddie—now a creepy beanie-wearing ghost—stored huge warehouse-store boxes of Pop Tarts. He sold the toaster pastries at exorbitant prices to local customers, who stood in line along Sunnyside Street. Laura, the girlfriend, collected their cash and did crowd control with a bullhorn.

The images left me with an unsettled feeling, and I jumped out of bed hoping that getting ready would clear them out of my head. I showered and dressed, then put Biga in his crate.

I left a note on the table telling my dad I was proud of him.

I didn't drive down Sunnyside that morning, just headed down Pilgrim to the main highway and into downtown. Once inside the bakery, I turned on the music and put Biga in his pen, then made him chase down one of his squeaky toys until I rewarded him with a liver treat.

As I checked loaves in the proofer, I thought back to my dream. Eddie had customers in the dream—just like he would have had in real life if Carleen's observations about his illegal operation were true. This meant there were

128

people in River Grove, and possibly in the Santa Cruz mountains, Santa Cruz, and in Los Gatos, who paid Eddie money for what he was dealing, whatever it was. We didn't know what this product or commodity was, but possibly hundreds of people out there did.

The question was, how could I reach them?

Chapter Sixteen

Wednesday—as I learned when the teenagers poured into the bakery at 7 a.m.—was Superhero Day for River Grove High's Spirit Week. Within five minutes the superhero universes congregated at the tables in the dining area, with Supermen, Wonder Women, a couple of Batmen, and about ten Spidermen, as well as a few other heroes wearing spandex leggings and capes. The idea behind the theme seemed to be that River Grove High's basketball team was so powerful, they were superhuman—how could they possibly lose this championship?

Chloe and many of the young women didn't dress up for this one, but Dakota Li was wearing a silver cape, tights, and silver cowboy boots. The silver cowboy boots had Elana's name written all over them.

When she came up to order, I asked where she'd gotten her outfit.

"Your superhero game is on point, Dakota." I smiled as I went to get her a cinnamon roll from the display case. "Where did you get those boots? They're amazing."

She smiled, then looked back at her friends at the large table. "Thank you, Gracie. They're—uh, designer."

I passed her the Cherry Orchard Latte Beck had just made for her. "Here you go. I have a friend who would love a pair of those. It's totally her style."

Dakota picked up her latte and gave me an odd, stunned look.

"I'm sorry, Gracie. They're not available anymore."

Dakota looked amazing, and that was not lost on Sky. He couldn't stop looking at her and managed to find a seat across from her at the big table, much to the chagrin of Dakota's friend, Amelia Gruber, who had to move her chair so he could fit in. She flashed Sky a dirty look.

When the line died down, Beck came over to me and smiled over at the noisy group of superheroes.

"I like this better than Crazy Hair Day. These kids are so creative with their costumes. That's one thing I missed being homeschooled," Beck said. "We never got to do things like this."

I gave her a wry smile. "Come on, Beck. You got to do classes in your pajamas."

Maeve came out and took some photos of the teenagers, who were all happy to pose for her.

When the clock hit 8:15 a.m., she got a group photo of the superheroes fleeing the bakery, looking like they were responding to a villainous attack just outside.

The Chief and Mayor C came up to the counter at 8:30 a.m., not long after the students had left. The Chief looked tired, and Mayor C looked lost in thought. Public safety was one of Mayor C's biggest concerns, and the fact that there was an unsolved murder in River Grove must be driving her crazy.

"What can I get you two? The usual?"

Mayor C nodded. "Same as always for me."

"Almond milk latte for me and the usual egg on toast, I guess."

"You know we're calling it 'The Chief' now, Dave."

"Really?" A smile spread across his face. "Well, I like that."

While they sat eating and discussing public safety strategies, I passed by their corner table.

"Anything new with the case?"

The Chief set his latte down. "I finally talked to Kirk Schiffer. He told me the whole story of Eddie Sumner and what happened at BlueSurf. What a mess. Eddie lied and strung the company along for a year, while saying he was working on the product. He cost the company a lot of money and opportunities, according to Kirk. Kirk came clean about the fact that he'd gone over and talked to Eddie the day of his murder. The thing is, Kirk *did* have a motive for killing Eddie. But he didn't do it."

While I was relieved to hear this, I wanted to know how the Chief had come to this conclusion.

"How do you know?"

"We just tracked down a neighbor who said he saw Eddie alive when he pulled into his driveway at 5:15 p.m.—after Kirk left. After yelling at Eddie, Kirk was back at Blue-Surf and meeting with his management team at 5:30."

I let out a sigh. Elana must be relieved.

"Nobody else on the list?"

The Chief looked up at me. "Carleen's not in the clear yet. She can't account for her time that evening. A janitor saw Laura Freitas working alone at her company offices that night, but the company is a small startup and there's no security desk. There's no time stamp of her hours that night."

Apart from Kirk being off the list of suspects, we were no closer to figuring out who killed Eddie Sumner.

"Chief, I was wondering about the illegal operation theory that Carleen told me about." I shot a look at his face to see that he was practically rolling his eyes. "What if Eddie was selling—dealing something out of his house. He could have been killed by a partner or by a rival seller."

"Gracie, you've helped with a few of our cases over the past two years. I've appreciated your help, but in this case, you've had the wool pulled over your eyes. You don't know this Fuller woman like we do."

The Chief turned away to continue his conversation with Mayor C, who frowned. She sat back and looked at me thoughtfully as the Chief continued talking.

I must have stomped back to the back room because Maeve looked up from shaping sourdough loaves and immediately asked me what was wrong.

"I love this town, but there's a stubbornness here that drives me crazy." I found the latte I'd started drinking earlier and took a gulp of the lukewarm liquid. "I'm frustrated, that's all."

"When I feel that way, kneading dough helps." Maeve looked up from the boules she was shaping. "There's some whole wheat dough left in the mixer if you want to knead it, old school."

"That's tempting," I said, frowning.

A conversation with Elana might work better. Now that Kirk was no longer a suspect, I'd check to see if I could stop by her house tonight to run some things past her.

I needed another session with my partner in crime.

Chapter Seventeen

After the Chief's dismissive comments about me, I didn't feel like talking to him—even though of course, I wanted to stay in the loop as far as the case was concerned.

When I'm upset about something, planning and organizing calms me down. I end up feeling more centered, more hopeful. It's the positive flip side of my need to problem solve.

At lunch, I set about working on how we'd set up a lunch menu and service at The Laughing Loaf.

We'd need to ramp up our bread production, which Maeve could be a big help with, if she intended to stay with The Laughing Loaf longer. We'd also need a meat slicer, as well as a new fridge dedicated to meats, produce and condiments for sandwiches. Our plucky 1960s aqua fridge—which Beck had dubbed The Little Fridge that Could—was adorable and a nice throwback to our building's past. But it didn't have the capacity for much other than a stash of beverages, drink additions, and the four different milks we offered customers for coffee drinks.

We were making a decent profit, which I could reinvest in the business.

I sketched out some possible expenses and considered that we'd need to hire on one or two employees to work the lunch shifts. We'd need to expand our front work area to accommodate those employees.

Preparing the bakery for this would be a lot of work—but it would be exciting work. Before I talked to Beck and Maeve, I wanted to have a plan sketched out for moving forward.

By the time I got back to work after this personal brainstorming session, I was feeling much better. I went back to have a cuddle session with Biga, then took him out for a short walk down the alley.

When I came back, I decided to see if I could get together one more time to talk to Carleen to ask her a question.

So I left a voicemail, even though it wasn't my preferred way of using my phone.

"Carleen. I wanted to ask you a question about your time working at Eddie's house. Can you give me a call back?"

Then I texted my partner in crime.

Got some time tonight? Can I swing by your place to chat? I need to pick your brain.

She must have been bored at work because I immediately got her response.

7 p.m. work?

My dad was tutoring Jeb tonight, so I made us a quick

dinner of fettuccine tossed with olive oil, herbs, and roasted vegetables.

My dad glowed again tonight, as he talked about tonight's lesson on momentum. I tried to focus on his explanation of Newton's second law, but physics was never really my interest, and my mind wandered. I hadn't gotten a message back from Carleen. The Chief hadn't updated me on the case today, and I was feeling like he'd told me this morning that my contributions were no longer needed.

"Are you doing all right, dear?" My father asked, between bites of fettuccine, and I suddenly realized I'd been staring off into space.

"Yeah. It's just that the Chief basically told me 'thanks for your help solving *some* of our cases, but we don't need you anymore.'"

"What? But you've helped him and the mayor on numerous cases. Why would he say that?"

"I suggested that we look into Carleen's theory that Eddie was selling illegal goods out of his house. And that maybe he was killed because of that." I couldn't eat any more of my pasta, so I set my fork down. "He told me that Carleen had fooled me, somehow tricked me into believing that's what happened."

My dad looked thoughtful and sat back in his seat. "So that's what Mary Jo was talking to you about."

"Mary Jo was defending her friend. A lot of people in River Grove think Carleen's not to be trusted. She stole something years ago. The woman's had a hard life and is struggling to make ends meet. I honestly don't see where she'd be making up this story about Eddie to somehow profit by it. Do you?"

My father took a sip of brandy. "I can't really see how it would be to her advantage."

"Now that the Chief is acting this way, it makes me want to figure this out even more."

My dad laughed into his glass. "Of course. That's how you've always been, dear. Just like your mother."

I looked up, startled. "Like mom? I don't remember her being like that." My memories of my mother were of a sweet, prim woman. Nice to everyone.

"She was a woman of quiet persistence. She found ways to make things work." My father's brown eyes looked moist as he remembered. "Shortly after we'd come over to the states from England, she spotted an apartment in Seattle that was perfect for us—close to the University for me, enough room for a piano for her. A lovely view across the Sound of the Olympic Mountains. It wasn't on the market. But she took walks past the place, met the landlord and his wife, and chatted with them whenever she saw them. She brought them scones she'd made. Almost a year later, the landlord told her he was renting out the place and if we wanted it, it was ours. We lived there till you started school."

I could picture the place, large and roomy, a beautiful view of the mountains. My bedroom was painted blue, my favorite color. There were lilac bushes outside my window. On warm spring days, when the windows were open, the deep, rich smell made me happy.

My dad got a distant look in his eyes.

"More than anything, your mother hated to give up. Even in those last days, when she was sick. You have that in you, Gracie."

I wondered what my mom would think of me if she could see me now. Running around this town solving murders. Maybe it's the kind of thing she'd have wanted to do.

I smiled. "That makes me feel good. Thanks, Dad."

He stood up and took his dishes to the sink, rinsed them, and put them into the dishwasher—just as I'd been tutoring *him* to do over the past two years. He adjusted his tweed jacket.

"Well, I'm going to print out a handout and pack up my case for tonight's lesson. I've got a lead on a new student who wants me to help her prepare for her AP test." The smile on his face was contagious. "I'm looking forward to working with her. Gracie, maybe you're right. This is only going to get better."

A little before 7 p.m., I packed Biga into his crate and took off for Elana's. It was a clear, cold night, and as I drove up the curve of Oceanview, lights twinkled in the far distance along the coast. I parked along the curb. When Biga and I walked up the steps, Elana let me in excitedly.

"Gracie, look at what Kirk got me." She spun around in her pink sequined bomber jacket. "Just arrived today. Isn't is gorgeous? It's like he read my mind."

I laughed to myself, as I remembered me giving Kirk that big hint the day before Valentine's Day. "Perfect for dancing. You and Kirk need a night out."

"We totally do!" She smiled at Kirk who was back in the kitchen. Kirk waved at me from the sink, just a little awkwardly. As soon as Biga saw Kirk, he trotted into the kitchen to spend time with his friend.

"Want something to drink? I've got a really good cab." Elana continued to twirl around, admiring herself, when she thought no one was looking, in nearby mirrors and reflective surfaces.

"I'll just have a glass of water, Elana. I've got to get up early."

In a few minutes, Kirk brought out a glass of wine for Elana and a tall glass of water for me.

He looked like a man with a new lease on life. He handed me my glass.

"Thanks, Gracie." He flashed me a grateful smile and gave me a side hug. "I'll leave you two. I've got a presentation to prepare for tomorrow in my office upstairs."

We sat on the comfy couches in the living room, looking out over the moonlit landscape outside. Elana wrapped her hands around her stemless wine glass.

"So what's up, girl? Kirk is *so* relieved right now. He's like a new man. I'm so glad that neighbor spotted Eddie alive after Kirk left. So who's on the hotseat now?"

I told her about what Carleen Fuller had said about Eddie running an operation on the side. Shipments coming in, people coming to the door to pick things up. I told her how the Chief had written off the idea of Eddie's illegal activity just because it came from Carleen.

"Do you or Kirk know anything about Carleen?"

"I don't, but Kirk grew up here. I didn't."

"The idea of Eddie having a business on the side makes sense to me. And it explains why Eddie was so flaky at work. His work at BlueSurf was actually his second job— and I bet he made a lot more money with his side gig. But the Chief and Brad searched Eddie's house and found nothing out of the ordinary. No rooms with boxes, like Carleen described."

Elana frowned. "So either Carleen was lying—or somebody came and took all the boxes."

Elana sat up and finally took off her sequined jacket, laying it reverently across the back of the couch. "You told me there was an intruder or intruders at the house when you drove by on your way to the bakery."

"For several days. Even the Chief and Brad saw someone run out of the house on their stakeout."

"But your problem is—" Elana took a sip of her cabernet. "There's nothing in the house right now that showed Eddie had the side business."

"And I don't even know what Eddie could have been selling. Was it drugs? Counterfeit electronics? Labradoodles? I have absolutely no idea what it could be. But… if he was selling these things, there are people in River Grove who bought from him. There has to be."

"And you're thinking that whoever might have been in this business with him killed him, to get more for themselves."

"Well, yes. I guess that is what I'm thinking."

We sat for a moment in silence, watching the branches on trees outside the window wave in the moonlight.

"What about the girlfriend? Lori? Laura or something?"

"Laura Freitas. I met her outside Eddie's house the day after he was killed."

"Maybe she was involved in the business with him. Maybe she killed him. Didn't you say he was kind of a bad boyfriend?"

"Yeah, I'd say so. She was supposedly working through the night on Valentine's Day at her company in San Jose. But it's a small startup and nobody was clocking when she came in or left."

"That's suspicious as hell." Elana lay back against the sofa and sipped her wine, sounding like a television detective. "So she's got no alibi."

"When Laura came in to talk to the Chief, she said she'd been in the process of breaking up with Eddie."

"You need to find out if Laura was involved in Eddie's business," Elana said firmly. "And really, you need to find out exactly what Eddie was selling. It's going to be hard to go anything further with this theory without knowing that."

"True, my friend." I finished the last of my water. "I know that's what I need to do. It's just that I have absolutely no idea how I'm going to figure that out."

But I was my mother's daughter.

I wasn't going to give up till I did.

Chapter Eighteen

I was back by 8:45 p.m., just in time to have a quick chat with Nate.

He was going stir crazy not being able to get out for his shoots, so he managed to hobble outside to his studio shed by the river to catch some local bird action.

"There was a turkey vulture by the river, so he must have spotted something small and injured. He was stunning, with that bright red head. I caught a few of his swoops."

He texted me two photos. On one he'd managed to get the arc of the bird's dive as it headed toward the riverbank, his enormous wings spread so I could see the details on the points of his feathers. The other showed the vulture approaching a fallen creature on the bank. The vulture's black, beady eye in his bright red bald head was intent on his fallen prey as he dove.

"These are fantastic, Nate. And also, creepy."

"It's how nature works. This guy needs to live just like any other creature in the woods. He's just more of an opportunist—preying on someone who's had bad luck."

"You're really good at this, you know."

He slid into his smooth jazz DJ voice. "I'm good at a *lot* of things. A little less than three weeks and I won't be an invalid. I can't wait till I'm able to be a little more... physical."

"*Okaaay*." I grinned and blushed a little. "Slow down there, tiger."

I updated Nate on the Eddie Sumner case, the Chief's dismissal of my idea, and my plan for going forward with my informal investigation.

"After talking to Elana, I've got some things to look into. I think Carleen was right. Eddie had a business of some kind. Now I just need to find his customers."

There was a pause. "Gracie, we've talked about this before. Be careful. Please?"

After a few reassurances—none of which seemed very convincing to Nate--we hung up.

❧

Students flooded into the bakery the next morning in tie-dyed t-shirts and bellbottom jeans —for 1970s Day—to commemorate River Grove High's founding in 1972.

I wondered what former hippie Reggie McFerrin would think of this, since he'd moved to town in the 1970s to found his commune, in the building that would become The Riverside Saloon.

Adults entered and lined up at the counter not long after the high schoolers left. The Chief and Mayor C were some of the first in line. The Chief clutched his portfolio of photos and case notes, which told me he was returning to square one on the Eddie Sumner case.

I didn't want to talk to the Chief or even see him today.

My voice of reason told me I needed to act like an adult and a responsible business owner. He was a customer, and I would provide him good customer service, even if I'd been hurt by what he'd said to me yesterday.

"The usual for you, Mayor C—and you Chief?"

"I'll have the apple tart today, Gracie," Mayor C said, as they looked over the display case.

"Give me drip coffee and the egg on toast today." The Chief refused to meet my eyes while talking and looked down at his feet and then into the dining area. I pulled out an apple tart and set it down on a plate.

"Great. And here are your coffees," I said, getting a little passive-aggressive with my perkiness. "That egg will be out in just a second. If you'd like to take your seats, I'll make sure you get it soon."

The mayor shot me a funny look, but then she and the Chief launched into a hushed conversation and made their way to their corner table.

The young dude who had fit right in with the teenagers last week came up to the counter, an easy grin on his face. He'd upgraded his Portland grunge look, and now he wore a stylish pair of what looked like designer black jeans with a retro yellow and blue knit shirt.

"Hey, Ezra, good to see you. What can I get you today?"

"I'll have a cappuccino, Gracie." He scanned the display case. "And one of those toaster pastries."

"How's life at BlueSurf?"

He shook his head, a sad look on his face. "Still crazy, trying to fix bugs in the Tsunami software. I hate to speak ill of the dead, but Eddie left us with a real mess."

At our lull time, at 10 a.m., the Chief and Mayor C were still at their table. The Chief was gesturing emphatically and pulling photos out of his portfolio. Mayor C sat back and crossed her arms, looking mildly disapproving or just bored. But of course, none of this was my business.

I went back to my office and checked my phone. I had a message from Carleen.

I clicked on the recorded voicemail and heard the folksy twang of Carleen's voice.

"You said you had some questions for me, hon? I'm downtown today. You wanna meet at 2:15?"

I responded to her voicemail with my own voicemail.

"Thanks, Carleen. Come to the bakery's back door. I'll see you then."

At lunch, I took Biga out for a short stroll to Grove Park, so he could get some exercise and have a chance to, well, pee. The walk to the park took us a while, since Biga was so excited to be sprung from his pen that he wanted to gleefully sniff every plant, hydrant, and pole on the way. It's as if he'd been released from a long prison term and wanted to savor everything around him.

We were walking across the park, and it had warmed up decently for a mid-February day. People sat on the benches lining the park's perimeter.

A familiar face looked up from a bench as we passed.

"Hey, Mary Jo." I called to her. She didn't look very excited to see me. She had a can of diet soda by her side and a slice of pizza from RG's on a paper plate on her lap, which made me feel sorry for her. I mean, she was a decent cook— so RG's Pizza? Really?

"Your father probably told you." The look on her face was grim. "We broke up."

Now I had no desire to meddle in my father's relationships. That seemed like a recipe for disaster, and more trouble than I needed in my life. I'd never been excited about Mary Jo's presence in my life or kitchen, but she seemed like a good person. So I thought I'd pass on what I'd heard from my dad.

"Actually, he said he *didn't* want to break up with you." I sat down next to her on the bench. "He wanted to slow things down. He's excited about tutoring, and he wants to include that and more time with his friends in his life."

She pursed her lips, skeptical. "I definitely got the feeling John was breaking up with me."

I felt like I was arbitrating a relational issue between two teenagers. My dad wasn't exactly a rockstar with social and emotional communication.

"I got the impression he really cares about you. But he wants to do other things, too. He's made some friends lately. And Reggie wants him to help put on a chess tournament at The Riverside."

"Really? I'm happy for him," Mary Jo said quietly. She studied my face, looking for clues. "We have been seeing an awful lot of each other. It's just that—well, it's been a year and a half since Bill died. We were married for thirty years. Eating dinner is so lonely. It's been nice to have that time with John." There was a hopeful look in her eyes. "But maybe he has a point. It doesn't have to be every night."

"I think that's what my dad was trying to say."

Biga was getting impatient with our conversation. He pulled on the leash, eager to move on.

She turned to me. "Gracie, I'm sorry I let loose on you about Carleen. She's been treated badly. I don't want to see things get worse for her."

"I'm glad you're watching out for her." I nodded. "I'd do the same for my friends."

Mary Jo brightened. She reached over to pat my hand. "Thanks for stopping to talk to me, hon. Your father has his head in the clouds most of the time. But I like him a lot."

. . .

At 2:15 p.m., I heard a tap on the bakery's back door. I led Carleen in, introduced her to Maeve and Beck, then we went into the dining area to talk.

"Carleen, would you like coffee? We have some cinnamon rolls left if you're hungry."

Carleen's eyes lit up. "Coffee would be great. Cinnamon rolls—really? Everyone in town tells me how good they are here."

I made her a latte and brought her a warmed-up cinnamon roll on a plate.

She must have been hungry because it took her about 60 seconds to devour it.

"I had a few questions for you, Carleen. Thanks for being willing to talk."

I'd been thinking about these for the past day, adding up what I knew about Eddie and what I didn't know but had traced an outline for, based on well... a lot of guessing.

"You talked about Eddie getting shipments at his house," I said, and Carleen nodded. "How often did he get them? Were they big boxes? Little boxes?"

She frowned as she thought. "He got a shipment of five or six big boxes, that I saw anyways. Like them big moving boxes. That's only when I was there, though."

"Did you see where they were from?"

She paused for a moment. "I had a quick look at one. Before Eddie moved it into the back bedroom. It had an address stamped on it. Somewhere in China."

"Any company name on it?" I asked. It was a long shot. I was digging for any personal or company name I could do a search for, to figure out what Eddie was dealing in.

Carleen shook her head. "I didn't get to see it before he

moved the box. I got the feeling I wasn't supposed to see it. And I didn't want to be let go."

"Did you see anyone else at Eddie's house during your cleaning? You said his girlfriend was there but didn't seem involved with the shipments."

Carleen shot a longing look at the display case. I wondered when she'd had her last meal, apart from the cinnamon roll.

"The Laura woman didn't look like she was doing anything with the shipments. And she didn't seem to care." Carleen shook her head. She picked pieces of caramelized cinnamon-brown sugar off her plate with gnarled, bony fingers. "I think Eddie's brother was there. I think it was his brother."

"What? Did you hear his name?" I hadn't heard of any relatives. The Chief had contacted Eddie's parents back east, but he hadn't said anything about local relatives. "Why did you think it was his brother?"

"They looked kind of alike. But I wasn't going to ask questions."

I sat and thought for a moment.

"Thank you, Carleen. I appreciate your help. I'd like to send something home with you."

When she stood up, I waved her over to the display case. "We usually take these home ourselves or sell them the next morning as day-olds. Let me know what you'd like, and I'll wrap it up."

Carleen's eyes got big. She got up and went to look at the display case. Her mouth turned up in a grin; she was a kid in a candy store.

"You mean it? Can I even take some things for Marisol and her kids?"

I nodded as I pulled out a big pink pastry box and set it

up for her, waiting for her choices. She ogled the case, pointing at scones, cinnamon rolls, tarts, and a few leftover beignets. Then she asked for a loaf of brioche. I boxed them all for her and gave her a large plastic bag to carry it in.

She reached out and shook my hand in an oddly formal gesture. "Thank you, Gracie."

Carleen was still smiling to herself—and looking a little like she'd gotten away with something—as she hurried with her bag of goodies to a rusted red Corolla parked on the street.

We'd been closed for an hour. Beck was rolling beignet dough, and Maeve was doing stretch and folds on tomorrow's sourdough loaves.

After I finished mixing cinnamon roll dough for tomorrow and set it in the fridge to chill, I decided to pay that visit to Key Haus, to ask if anyone had come in to have keys made that could have been for Eddie's house.

"I'm walking down to Key Haus," I called out to Beck and Maeve. "I won't be long."

I put Biga's leash on him and bundled up in my warm jacket.

We walked down to Key Haus, located on the other side of Speed Spot Motors. The shop was ancient; the small brick building dated back to the 1920s, just like the original bank building that was now The Laughing Loaf. Key Haus had a steepled wooden chalet façade attached to its roof that made it look like it belonged in Bavaria. The Shulz family had owned the shop for generations and had originally come from Germany. Two brothers in their late 70s now ran it—Hank and Victor.

I'd been in the shop two years ago when I'd had keys made for our house after moving in.

The bell on the door tinkled when I entered the shop, which was lined with multiple racks of colorful key options hanging on hooks, bins of key chains and framed photos of local dignitaries from long ago. The shop smelled pleasingly like dust, old wood, and metal. A signed photo was posted on the wall, yellowed with age, of a very young-looking Scotty Baxter, famed winner of the 1986 River Grove Chili Cookoff.

An older man in a sweater with a very full white moustache came out to the counter.

"You're Gracie from the bakery, aren't you? We're big fans of your cinnamon rolls. I'm Hank Schulz."

When I had keys made for my house, I must have talked to Victor." I smiled. "I had a question for you. Did somebody come in around Valentine's Day, asking to have keys made for a front door lock, a deadbolt, and a sliding door?"

Hank tapped the counter as he thought. "If it was last week, it would be Victor. I was in Arizona visiting the grandkids. If it was this week, it would have been me. Why don't you tell me what you need? I'll see what I can find out."

"I want to know if the keys were made here, and if you can tell me who had them made. Someone's been getting into Eddie Sumner's house."

"And his murder's still not solved." He shook his head and paused, in thought. He turned to an enormous beige computer monitor and started tapping on a keyboard. The chunking noise of the keyboard reminded me of a computer my father had when I was in elementary school.

"I'll need to look up any sales we had for a batch of those keys. I didn't handle anything like that this week, but

I'll check our records to be sure. If I can find it, I should be able to pinpoint the day, which might help me or Victor remember who made the purchase."

I handed him a Laughing Loaf business card with my cell phone number written on the back.

'If you do remember, please give me a call. Thank you, Hank."

After we left the shop, I walked past The Riverside Saloon. I didn't see Reggie McFerrin himself, but I did see Drake, the bartender, heading for the main doors. Four months ago, the man's quick actions saved my life. I called out to him, and he waved at us.

"Well, Biga boy, let's head back—" Then I stopped suddenly.

I noticed something across the street, on the corner near RG's Pizza.

I was confused by what I was seeing.

Someone familiar, looking down at his phone. He was not much taller than I was. A shiver rippled through me.

I was looking at a dead man.

Chapter Nineteen

At a distance, with his height, his movements, and the black beanie he was wearing, I swore I was looking at Eddie Sumner.

The man put his phone in his back pocket, looked around him, and continued along the sidewalk into downtown.

Biga and I followed him at a distance. My dog was confused as to where we were going, since we weren't heading toward The Laughing Loaf.

I kept half a block behind the man, following him as he turned a corner to the parking lot behind City Hall and the cleaners. He approached a white BMW and clicked a fob to unlock the door.

I had to get the license plate number.

As he backed out of the space, I half jogged, pretending my dog was pulling on the leash. *What the hell, woman?* Biga turned around and gave me a weird look, then obligingly sped up.

I was able to get close enough to snap a slightly unsteady photo of the back of the car as it headed for the exit on the side street.

Got it.

My heart pounding, I turned onto a side street and found the alley, continuing my fast pace until I got to the back steps of my bakery.

I popped into the bakery's back room and told Beck I'd be right back. Then I crossed the street to City Hall.

My nemesis, young City Hall receptionist Peony Roberts, sat primly at her desk. Today she'd braided her hair and wound the braids into loops pinned to the sides of her head. It was an interesting effect—if she'd been wearing a shawl, she'd look like Marmee, the beloved mother in Louisa May Alcott's *Little Women*.

"I need to see the Chief," I announced.

Peony was in the process of assessing me for entry to the offices in the back when her phone rang.

"He's just getting back from his meeting with the county sheriff, Gracie. One moment—"

She answered the phone and lifted a finger, signaling for me to wait.

I saw my chance. I barreled down the hall into the cluster of offices, looking for the Chief.

Instead, I found Mayor C, sitting at her computer. She stood up in surprise.

"Gracie, what's up?"

"I'm looking for the Chief. I have something to tell him, assuming he'll even listen to me. I need him to look something up for the Eddie Sumner case. A license plate number. I have an idea, but I want to be sure."

She was thoughtful for a moment. At first, I thought she'd demand a detailed explanation; the mayor seemed determined to involve herself in town law enforcement, whether it was her job or not. The woman had one of the most serious cases of FOMO I'd seen.

She paused for a moment. "We don't have any other leads right now. I'm going to trust you on this, Gracie, because of your track record. The Chief may not."

I sank down into the chair in front of her desk and groaned. "Why is the Chief being so dismissive of me? And why doesn't he trust anything Carleen Fuller says?"

The mayor sat back in her chair and looked thoughtful. "The Chief isn't a River Grove native, but he's tried very hard to act like one. He's accepted what people in town have been saying about Carleen for years. They see her as an outsider—and it's easier to think of her that way than try to get to know her. Or help her."

She pulled out her cell phone and pressed speed dial.

"Dave, Gracie's here with me. She needs you to look something up." She gave me an assessing look. "I'll put you on speaker phone."

"I have a possible suspect in the Eddie Sumner case." I leaned forward as I said it, as if that little lean would help me come through better on speaker phone. "I believe this guy is involved in whatever's going on in Eddie Sumner's house. I'd like you to look up his license plate number."

I heard the Chief sigh heavily. There was a pause on the line.

"Give me the number. I'll check it out."

I pulled out my phone and scrolled to the photo of the license plate. It was blurry but still readable.
"Come by the bakery when you get in—and I'll explain."

Chapter Twenty

I walked with Biga down the alley then up the steps to The Laughing Loaf.

The pieces were falling into place.

I saw how clueless I'd been.

That black beanie.

Now I understood how people could be completely baffled that Clark Kent and Superman were the same person.

Put the glasses on, you have Clark Kent.

Put the black beanie over Ezra's spiky, hip hair and you had someone who looks like Eddie Sumner.

I was pretty sure the man Carleen thought was Eddie's brother was Ezra, Eddie's fellow BlueSurf employee.

Ezra had Eddie's height and build. It would make sense that he was the one who'd been in Eddie's house on those early mornings, probably moving the shipments somewhere else. He'd presumably had keys made at Key Haus. Maybe he'd had them duplicated from Laura's or from Eddie's set of keys.

I went through my mental list of what I knew and what I didn't. I might have made a few leaps here.

<u>Possible murderer?</u> Ezra. He'd been seen at Eddie's house—probably the "brother" Carleen said she'd seen helping with the shipments and pickups.

<u>His motive?</u> Cutting in on Eddie's profitable business. Eddie must have been making a good amount of money with his side business and he'd neglected his work as lead architect of BlueSurf's new Tsunami product. When Eddie was forced to set aside his second job for the deadlines of his BlueSurf job, Ezra moved in to take over Eddie's business and kill him. Just as Nate's turkey vulture swooped in on the injured animal on the riverbank.

<u>What was Eddie dealing?</u> I HAVE NO IDEA! Something from China.

That's where I hit the roadblock. I didn't know what Eddie was dealing in. And without knowing that, it was going to be hard to solve this case. I suspected it was illegal drugs or goods, but beyond that I knew nothing. And since these unknown goods were missing, how would I ever find out what they were?

Back at The Laughing Loaf, my head buzzed with excitement, and the emptiness in my stomach made me feel queasy. I hadn't eaten all day. I went to the stash of rye I'd baked last week, cut myself a slice, then spread it with cream cheese. I closed my eyes in bliss. It hit the spot.

"The dining area's emptying out." Beck came in from the front area with a bussing bin full of cups and plates. She set them down by the dishwasher and studied me. "Is something going on, Gracie? You have that look. Like you're really, really focused on something."

"I am. I'm just about to talk to the Chief about it."

She looked at me slyly. "For a while you said you

weren't interested in the case, Gracie. But I had a feeling you'd end up working on it."

I shrugged and smiled. "And you were right. I got sucked in, as usual."

While I waited for the Chief to come over, I went to my office and reviewed a quote I'd received for modifying The Laughing Loaf's front area for lunch service. Then I mixed up a double batch of cinnamon roll dough, based on a quick check of tomorrow's cold weather forecast.

At 3:45 p.m., I heard a tap at the back door. I let the Chief and Mayor C in, and we moved to the corner table in the dining area. The Chief frowned as he sat down across from me. He opened a folder and took out a printout and a page of written notes.

"I hope this isn't some wild goose chase, based on what that Fuller woman told you."

He ran a finger down his page of notes. "The car's registered to an Ezra Dupont, age 27. He moved here to River Grove last fall for a programming job in Santa Cruz."

"Yes, when he came into the bakery, he talked about it." I sat up. I remembered when the guy had come into The Laughing Loaf, and he'd blended in so well with the high schoolers, he could have been their age. "He works for BlueSurf."

"I have no reason to question this guy, Gracie. Was he friends with Eddie Sumner? Was he seen in Eddie's house on the day Eddie was killed?"

I thought about this quickly. If I said I got this info from Carleen, the Chief would discount it. "Yes, he was seen in Eddie's house. And he is about the same height as the guy I saw in the windows when I drove past in the early morning last week."

I was 98 percent sure of it, anyway.

"I'll contact Ezra Dupont and ask him to come in." He nodded, his face serious. "At this point, we're looking for any new angle on the case. I sure hope this pans out." He looked back at his printout. "By the way, Ezra's your neighbor. He lives on Pilgrim Way."

AFTER THE CHIEF and Mayor C left, I went in the back room and put Biga in his pen with some new water in his bowl. He drank from it, then curled up on his blanket. It had been a busy day for both of us, and he needed a nap. Of course, I did, too, but I wasn't going to get one.

An Irish playlist on the sound system filled the back room with music. Maeve was sliding pans with sourdough loaves into the oven.

Beck was still in the front, making coffee drinks since we had an hour to go before closing.

I went to work on scones, which I'd roll out and freeze for tomorrow: I'd been playing with new scone flavors and had decided to try an ube and golden raisin scone, in honor of River Grove High's school colors. Since River Grove's big game was Friday night, it would be fun to surprise the teens with the delicious flavor and gorgeous purple color from Filipino purple yams—topped with golden raisins.

For now, this would be a limited menu item, for just the next week. Ube brought a delicate, nutty and creamy flavor, and the purple color alone would sell these scones.

I mixed up the dough, then rolled it out, sprinkling it with frozen butter I'd grated. Then I began laminating—creating the layers—by rolling out the dough and butter, then folding it over. When these were baked, the butter would melt and create flaky layers.

The repeated rhythm of turning the dough and rolling

it, turning it and rolling it, kept me calm as I thought of how blind I'd been about the Eddie-Ezra connection.

Soon I had a tidy stack of uniform, purple dough-and-butter layers. I cut the dough into triangles and laid them out on baking sheets for tomorrow morning. Then I stacked the sheets in the freezer.

Tonight, I'd make dinner for my dad and I—filling in on a night originally scheduled for my dad and Mary Jo to make dinner. My dad had hinted he was inviting a "special guest." I was hoping this wasn't going to be a *Psych! Mary Jo's baaaaack* kind of situation. In my opinion, they needed time apart to think about things.

I was curious about our guest, but it had also been a long day and I was tired. I'd planned to make a dish my mom had made when I was growing up: chicken curry with rice, peas, and homemade naan. It was homey and satisfying, and that's exactly what I needed right now. The dish brought up so many memories for me. It was comforting to smell the familiar spices and ingredients again.

Since we ate on the early side, I told Nate I'd bring him a wrapped-up portion after we finished.

I sliced up chicken breasts, while my father put together a study plan for Mila Benson, his new student for AP Physics prep. He'd have his first meeting with her tomorrow night, and he couldn't stop talking about it.

"Her parents told me she's quite advanced. She's planning on a career in engineering. I'm trying to figure out if I should just lay out a curriculum based on what she'll find on the test or if I should assess where she's at—then proceed."

"I think it's always good to meet somewhere where they're at, Dad." I watched as he leafed through handouts, pulling a few of them out. "Also, everyone learns differently. Maybe meet her first."

"Right. Brilliant idea, dear."

"Looks like dinner will be ready at 6:15. When's our special guest arriving?" I was getting curious. And a little nervous.

"Our guest will be here at around 6 p.m.," my father said mysteriously. I had some worries since he wasn't indicating a gender. I really hoped it wasn't Mary Jo, but it could be anyone in town whom my Dad chatted with. Once he got out of his world of theories and equations, he could be a very chatty guy.

I was flipping the homemade naan and waiting for the rice to finish when the doorbell rang. After the craziness of last fall when we had some unwanted Russian visitors, I'd installed a doorbell camera. I wanted to make sure we knew who was on our doorstep. My dad peered at the camera.

"He's here!" He called out and opened the door.

I heard the voice of one of my favorite River Grove residents—Reggie McFerrin. I could call Reggie a friend, but so could almost everyone in River Grove who'd met him.

When I'd first met Reggie, I'd been a little afraid of him. With his dark clothes and pale skin, he looked like a hippie vampire. I soon got to know him, even become his friend. He had the easygoing, carefree attitude of The Dude in *The Big Lebowski* movie--combined with the goofy wisdom of Tom Bombadil in *The Lord of the Rings* books.

I quickly wiped the naan flour off my hands and went out to meet him. Biga was already there, putting his paws up on Reggie's legs.

He was wearing a dialed-down version of his standard wear—a black t-shirt under a black suit coat with black jeans —and an interesting new touch, suspenders. I could see his eyes behind his shaded glasses.

I hugged him. "I had no idea you were coming, Reggie." I smiled.

"I hope that's not a problem," he said with a wry smile, looking at my dad. "John and I are going to play chess. And talk about the tournament I want to have at The Riverside this summer. I'm honored to have John work with me on this."

"I know he's very excited about it." Reggie was the one chess player in River Grove who could beat my dad. That instantly earned him my dad's respect.

I let out a little yelp when I smelled the distinct scent of charred naan and ran back into the kitchen.

After dinner, I texted Nate to tell him I was almost on my way. I packed curry, rice and naan in insulated containers, then I hugged Reggie and my dad and took off for Nate's.

I'd been telling myself not to go down Sunnyside, since it tended to be frustrating and pointless. Especially if all the goods Eddie had been dealing were long gone. But old habits die hard. There was a lure there for me that I can't explain. Like the house itself was a keeper of a mystery, and I was going to keep returning to it until it spilled its secrets.

I turned onto Sunnyside and drove in the direction of his house. There were no lights on this stretch of the street and the moon was a mere sliver in the sky—so no help there.

I parked on the opposite side of the street, right behind a pickup truck. Then I got out and quietly padded across the street to the house. My eyes became accustomed to the dark pretty fast, and I was able to see more than I could in my car.

I approached the left side of the house, which would be the living room. This is where I'd seen a figure behind the blinds last week.

I walked across the front of the house, peering into the windows. The windows in the living room and the first bedroom were covered by blinds that were slightly open, so I could see the rooms inside in thin strips. The living room was dark, but a hall light was on, and it cast some light on the room. I made out the shapes of a sofa, a big screen TV hanging on the wall, and a bookshelf.

The bedroom was harder to see since the door was shut and there was no light in the room at all. I continued moving along the front of the house. And then I heard it. The click of a deadbolt. Then the creak of a door opening.

Adrenaline shot through my body, and I ran. I sprinted across the lawn of the house next door, then crouched behind a garbage can next to the neighboring house's garage, trying to catch my breath.

A gunshot rang out in the cold night air.

Chapter Twenty-One

Since I had my phone with me, I texted the Chief and Brad.

I told Nate I'd be a few minutes late.

Neighbors in the surrounding houses who'd heard the shot came out of their front doors and huddled on their front porches.

In five minutes, Deputy Brad Castro's truck pulled up in front of the house where I was hiding. Ten minutes later, the Chief pulled up in the RGPD squad car, lights flashing.

"It was a warning shot," I said, as I shivered from the shock and from spending the past twenty minutes in the cold. "It wasn't aimed in my direction. Whoever fired did it to scare me off."

"Brad and I are going to search the house and yard, Gracie." The Chief gave me a stern look. "I'm not going to ask you tonight why you happened to be here. We'll talk tomorrow. Now please go."

As the Chief and Brad approached the house, I did as he told me, got in my car and left.

. . .

NATE LET me in from the cold, a worried look on his face.

I should have known he'd hear about it.

"Brad told Sam that you were shot at." His face was white. "Sam just called. Gracie, what the hell happened?"

I went into the kitchen and put the bag with his dinner on the counter.

We sat down on the sofa, and he held me.

"I drove past Eddie's house on the way here," I said, continuing to shiver. "Maybe it sounds strange, but I just couldn't help myself. This has been driving me crazy for a week. I wanted to look in the windows. I wanted to see that the Chief was right—the place had been cleared out. I didn't see anyone inside—and I didn't expect anyone would be there. As I was looking in the window, I heard the front door open, so I ran to the neighbor's house and hid behind their trash cans. That's when I heard the shot."

Through my explanation, Nate's face had gone from worry to puzzlement to frustration.

"Gracie, this was dangerous." Despite his stoic face, I knew he was scared. And a little mad at me. "Why did you do this?"

He was worried about my safety and probably about my decision-making. It was not the time to bring it up—but a few months ago, he'd fallen off a cliff in the Galapagos Islands while trying to photograph a finch at the perfect angle. Was this *that* different?

"I'm so close to figuring out why Eddie Sumner was killed. I think I know who did it, and why. But I don't know the whole story. It's going to bug me till I figure it out."

Nate sighed and threaded his fingers through mine. When he turned his blue eyes on me, I knew he was struggling with anger—and fear. But when he spoke, his voice was calm and soft.

"Why don't you tell me what you know so far?"

I told him about my sighting of the Eddie lookalike on the street—and the vehicle's registration to Ezra Dupont. And my trip to the key shop, where I suspected Ezra had gotten keys to go back to the house and remove the goods.

"Still don't know what the goods are, though." Why was this part so hard to figure out? I felt like I was so close. It was right under my nose.

"Eddie worked in tech." Nate thought about this. "Maybe he re-sold electronics or chips. You said the boxes were from China—there could be a connection for tech components there. Or maybe something like bootleg video game equipment?"

"I guess that's possible." That made sense with Eddie's employment and his tech background. I can't believe I didn't think of the electronics angle. "I'll do some research into that."

Nate kissed the side of my head.

"I know how much you love doing this, Gracie. I can't tell you not to do it. Just, please, be careful. You're tracking a killer. Somebody who's crossed the line and killed someone won't have problems doing it again."

Turns out I didn't have to wait till tomorrow for the Chief to talk to me.

As soon as I got back in my car to drive home from Nate's, he called.

"Gracie, first of all—what did you think you were doing at Eddie Sumner's house? By yourself?"

"I just heard all this from Nate, Chief." I said, shivering in my cold car outside Nate's house. "I just got curious."

"Let Brad and I do the work," the Chief said sternly. "Will you promise me you won't do this again?"

Well, not specifically this *thing.*

I changed the subject.

"There was somebody inside, Dave. Somebody who had keys to get in." I hoped I'd get confirmation of the sale and a description of Ezra tomorrow from Hank Shulz at Key Haus.

The Chief grunted. "At least now we know. Somebody is either living at the house or coming by to visit it. And they're willing to shoot at anyone they think is a threat."

"You didn't find anything on your search tonight?" Whoever was in the house could have gotten careless and left some trace of their presence.

"Nothing we didn't see before," the Chief said. "We could have crime scene come in to sweep again for hair and fingerprints, but I don't think it's worth it."

After all we'd gone through in the past couple of days, since I had him on the phone, I wanted to bring up his dismissive attitude toward me in The Laughing Loaf. I knew I needed to let go of it, but it still really bugged me.

"Chief, why did you treat me the way you did at the bakery yesterday? You know, when I brought up Carleen's theory of Eddie running an illegal business out of his home."

"Come on, Gracie." The Chief groaned. "You've helped me out a lot over the past two years. But you move into our town and think you're smarter than the rest of us. You don't know Carleen like I know her, like the old timers in this town know her. The woman lives hand to mouth. She's a scavenger. She will do whatever she can to survive. And if that means telling a good story to protect herself, she'll do it."

I thought about the glee in her eyes as she loaded up on baked goods from the case today at The Laughing Loaf.

"Gracie, it looks like she's fooled you good."

Chapter Twenty-Two

Friday morning, I had to drag myself out of bed.

It was 3:40 a.m., ten minutes past my usual weekday wake-up time because I'd hit the snooze button. Every muscle in my body ached.

Was a quick run across a lawn too much exercise for my out-of-shape body?

Biga had already gotten up and defected to my dad's room.

I herded myself into the shower, got dressed and prepared to go to work. If it was going to be a busy day, with a few trips across the street to City Hall and maybe to the key shop, it made sense to leave Biga at home with my dad.

I drove to the bakery, avoiding Sunnyside today.

I shivered as I came in the back door. I hated to turn on the heat at the bakery—because *money*—but I did it, just to warm things up for a few minutes. Once we started baking, the back room would feel cozy.

I did a run-through of the bakery. Loaves in the proofer; tart shells baked and ready to fill. Beignet dough and fillings all set to assemble. I'd filled and baked chocolate hazelnut toaster pastries for today, and there were scones in the freezer to bake. Even with the disruption yesterday afternoon of tracking down Ezra Dupont, we'd prepped everything we needed for this morning.

I started the coffeemaker in the back room, just to make something warm to drink. It was still pre-coffee to me. But it would warm me up and caffeinate me until Beck could make me a decent latte, and that's what I needed this morning.

With all that would happen today, I'd need a lot more caffeine to keep up.

Beck came in, wrapped in a scarf, a beret on her head.

"Gracie! I'm so glad to see you! I heard about last night."

"It wasn't one of my better ideas. I was curious, so I went to check out Eddie Sumner's house, on my way to Nate's." I smiled at her reassuringly. "The shot didn't come anywhere near me. I think someone was trying to scare me away."

"Who could still be living in the house?" She hung up her hat and scarf on the rack and went to wash her hands. "That's really spooky."

"I have an idea as to who it could be." I poured her and me a cup of from the coffeemaker. "I'm just not sure *why* they're there."

Maeve came in at 6:30 a.m., also bundled up. She'd heard last night's news from Mayor C. "Corinne was up late last night. She was talking to the Chief about it till 10. I honestly didn't think she was capable of staying up that late." She came up and gave me a hug. "So glad you're okay, Gracie."

Today was School Color Day at River Grove High School so at 7 a.m., the high schoolers came in with purple and gold clothes, makeup, hair, hair accessories, socks and shoes. Excitement had been building as the week progressed toward Friday's big game. Even students who could not care less about their school's sports teams were dressing up.

Compared to the rest of the week's themes, wearing the school colors was a low bar—every River Grove student had at least a set of PE clothes in the school colors.

The room was a sea of purple and gold. When the students saw the purple ube scones in the display case, several teens squealed.

"OMG! Purple? They're so pretty, Gracie!"

After students plunked their bags down on the tables and jumped into the line at the counter, I looked back at the large table and suddenly saw something I'd never seen before.

Or maybe I had *seen* it before, but in the rush of serving the high schoolers in the mornings—and doing crowd control—I just hadn't noticed.

Across the table, strewn haphazardly by teens dropping them in a hurry, were at least a dozen purses, handbags, backpacks and totes with designer labels. I'm not talking about items from stores in Santa Cruz or San Jose where River Grove students typically shopped for school clothes and accessories for the school year.

These were high-end, expensive fashion labels. Prada, Gucci, Coach, Burberry, and Marc Jacobs. I wasn't a fashion expert by any means, and I depended on Elana for my fashion advice. But I knew these weren't brands students in small town River Grove could afford. Something was wrong with this picture.

Still, I kept filling orders and handing over espresso drinks. I couldn't press pause on this situation to try to figure out the significance of what I'd just seen.

But when Sky Robbins came into the bakery, dressed in his PE clothes and a purple top hat, I looked him over, and I saw what I'd seen that night of Eddie Sumner's murder.

Sky sitting on Eddie's steps, his long skinny legs ending in a pair of large, high-top Nike Jordans.

Very expensive shoes I knew neither Sky nor his family could afford.

"Sky, I need to talk to you. Now."

Maeve had just come up front from the back room. I waved her over and had her take over for me at the counter.

I pulled Sky into the back room. He looked scared.

"Sky, I want you to tell me where you got those shoes."

He swallowed hard and I could see the wheels turning in his head. He was nervous and trying hard to think of something funny to diffuse the tension, but it wasn't coming to him.

"Before you made the delivery to Eddie's on Valentine's Day, you had gone there before."

Sky hesitated then nodded. He took in a deep breath.

"Yes. Dakota and me both." He was turning pale. "Somebody at school told us you could get cheap, cool shoes at his place. There was a website with a fake name—Miss Dottie's Yarn Emporium—and you would put in your order there. Then at certain pickup times, early in the evening, you could go by and get your stuff."

"But they were knock-offs. Counterfeit designer shoes."

"Yeah, and purses and stuff. It looked pretty legit, too. I mean, he had a lot of cool shoes, and I could afford them." He smiled weakly. "I usually can't."

"Why didn't you tell anybody that night at Eddie's house? That you knew him?"

He looked down at the floor. "I knew we did something bad, buying the stuff. I knew the stuff was probably illegal.

When we picked up the shoes, we were told we could tell other students, but no adults. If we told anybody else, they'd come after us."

"Eddie told you that?"

"Not him. Another guy. Blond hair, short guy."

"His name was Ezra?"

He nodded.

"You know the Chief will need to talk to you."

"Yeah, I know." Sky's face was red with shame. "Maybe I'll see if I can talk to Seth about it first."

"Good idea, Sky."

After this, I texted the Chief and told him I'd found out something about Eddie, but I couldn't talk to him till mid-morning.

Eddie Sumner had been selling counterfeit designer goods on the side. But in order to make it worth his while—since he was taking away from his day job at BlueSurf—he couldn't just sell to River Grove High School students. To make a bigger profit, he must have been selling to other teens in the area. I thought about what Sky said, about Ezra threatening the teens not to tell adults.

The business had intentionally targeted customers who would be less likely to go to the police.

I had even more questions now.

Still, I had a bakery to run.

Since I couldn't desert my bakery now, I needed to call Key Haus to see what Hank had found out from the sales records. I wanted to confirm that Ezra had come in to have keys to Eddie's house made.

After the high schoolers had left, and things had settled in with the adult crowd, I called Hank.

"Gracie, I did find that receipt in the book. Victor and I talked, and he remembers the customer. She came in right when we opened at 9, the day after Valentine's Day. She actually had four different keys made. One was a smaller key, and neither of us are sure what that one was for."

"Wait. You said *she*?"

My thoughts jumped to Carleen. Had I been duped somehow, like the Chief had said?

Then he responded.

"A young woman. Victor says she was dressed like a fashion model. Her name's Laura."

Apparently, before turning her keys in to the Chief that day, she'd made copies for herself.

Laura, and anyone else who needed to, would have had no problems getting back into the house.

Laura Freitas was now involved in Eddie's illegal operation.

And possibly his death.

Chapter Twenty-Three

At 10:15 a.m., I walked across the street to City Hall to tell the Chief what I'd learned this morning.

Peony Roberts gave me the stare of death as I entered.

"Gracie, you do know this is a government office. Do you have *so* little respect for authority that you just walk right past me?"

She was right. But I was, as always, in a hurry. I took a deep breath, trying to calm myself down. "Peony, when I come over here to talk to the Chief or Mayor C, I've only got a few minutes to spare. The Chief and mayor usually know I'm coming. Not trying to disrespect your authority. I just can't wait."

Peony curled her lip in a look of utter scorn, as if she'd lost any remaining respect for me.

Then she ran a finger down the calendar on her desk. She sighed heavily. "The Chief is in for the next hour. I *suppose* you can go back."

"Wait, what? Uh, *fine*." I mumbled, rolling my eyes as I hurried down the hall to The Chief's office.

The Chief was typing something on his computer when I walked in.

He didn't look up.

"Come on in, Gracie." He raised his hand and gestured vaguely toward a chair near the door of his office. "Have a seat."

He finally looked up after I'd pulled over the old captain's chair and sat down in front of his desk.

"Eddie—and possibly his girlfriend Laura and coworker Ezra—were running a counterfeit designer goods business. River Grove High School students, and I'm sure students from other schools in the area, bought from him on a regular basis. I estimate a third of the teens coming into my bakery bought his knockoff designer handbags, backpacks and shoes. That's judging by what I saw on the tables in the bakery this morning."

"What the hell?" The Chief frowned, and his eyes narrowed. "What proof do you have that this has been going on, Gracie?"

I nodded. "This morning, Sky Robbins admitted he'd met Eddie before the night of his murder. When he picked up his Air Jordan athletic shoes."

The Chief pushed away from his computer. He snorted out a laugh. "Even I know the kid can't afford those."

"Exactly. None of the teens who bought these fake designer goods could afford the real thing. So they bought from Eddie. He operated a website masquerading as a yarn store. Kids could order what they wanted, then pick it up at his house."

The Chief shook his head. "Sky's willing to talk to me?"

"He's running what he's going to say past Seth Gordon. I bet there are other teens who will talk, too. They'll want to know they won't get in trouble."

The Chief grunted. "Okay, so that's one thing. But who killed Eddie? That's what we really need to know."

"You need to talk to Ezra and to Laura Freitas." I continued, telling him about the key situation. "Right before she turned in the keys to you and Brad on February 15th, Laura had four keys duplicated at Key Haus. A front door key, back door key, sliding door key—and one unidentified key. Hank Schulz said it was for a small lock assembly. The kind you'd use for a cupboard."

The Chief leaned his chair back on two legs. It always made me nervous since I expected him to fall backwards and crack his skull. I'd come to know, this dangerous position just meant he was in thinking mode.

"Gracie, is the fake website still up?"

I'd heard the name from Sky—Miss Dottie's Yarn Emporium. I Googled it.

An illustration appeared—the face of a grey-haired, bespectacled old lady, surrounded by knitting needles and yarn.

Under SHOP were headings for Yarn, Needles, Patterns, and Accessories. When I clicked these headings, I saw listings for designer athletic shoes, handbags/backpacks, boots, and clothing.

I nodded at the Chief. "It's up and running."

The Chief picked up his cell phone and pressed speed dial.

"Yeah, Brad? Gracie's here. We've got a lead in the Sumner case. When do you get off at Best Buy?" The Chief tapped something into his tablet. "Come on by my office then. We need to come up for a plan for tonight."

I looked down at my phone to check the time. I needed to be back at the bakery.

"Chief, I have a feeling the merchandise is still somewhere on Eddie's property. I think that's why someone was at the house when I looked in the windows." My stomach was getting fluttery. We could be getting close to a solution in this case. "I suspect Ezra and Laura are still doing business."

"Well, good." I saw the beginnings of a smile on the Chief's face. "Let's catch them in the act and see what we can find out."

Chapter Twenty-Four

Once I walked through the front door of The Laughing Loaf, I got back to work.

A big chunk of my life in the past week and a half had been taken up with the Eddie Sumner case. I enjoyed figuring out a puzzle, but I had a business to run.

While I was with the Chief, Beck and Maeve had worked together to man the front counter and continue prepping and baking in the back room. At 1:20 p.m., business was slowing down, and we'd close at 2 p.m. There was no line. A few customers sat at the tables sipping coffee drinks while working on their laptops or having quiet conversations.

"Thanks, you two." I nodded at Beck, who was wiping down the coffee area. Maeve was replenishing the display case with half a tray of ube scones and had put out the last of our chocolate hazelnut toaster pastries.

"Something's up." Beck looked up from the espresso machine with interest. "You were talking to the Chief for a long time."

"I can't say much about it, but it looks like we're closing

in on the killer. And figuring out what was going on at Eddie's house."

"Fair play, Gracie." Maeve raised an air high-five in my direction. She explained to me once that this was Irish slang for, "You did good."

Beck sighed as she knocked a round of espresso grounds into the trash. "I'll be relieved when this is all over."

Maeve paused at the door of the back room, her forehead crinkling. "I didn't know I was working in such a dangerous town. I'd never guess that based on the friendly people I've met here." She smiled softly. "There are times when I think, if I didn't have a boyfriend and another job in Napa, I could live here permanently."

"Please don't judge River Grove by what's been going on with the Eddie Sumner case," Beck said. "I grew up here. There's no place more beautiful than River Grove. People in our town help each other out."

"Besides, Mayor C is going to make sure nothing happens to you in her care," I said with a grin. "If I were a murderer, I would not want to come up against her."

I sat down in front of the computer in my little office and went through emails. Two of the remodeling companies I'd talked to had come up with quotes and a preliminary design of how they'd approach converting the front area to accommodate lunch service.

One plan retooled the counter area into an oval island with a smooth white composite top, with seats at the counter and a sandwich prep station. There were pay stations and an espresso machine in the middle area, facing customers as they came in the door. In the other plan, the front had a long, rustic wooden counter, almost freestanding, divided into a coffee service area and a lunch ordering area.

Both were affordable, but I wanted to think about this. I wanted to introduce the idea to Beck and Maeve and get their input before I went any further with it.

After closing up, we went to work on prep for the next day. With 80s music playing and all of us singing along, I fell into my routine.

I knew the Chief was going to get back to me with a plan for dealing with Ezra Dupont and Laura Freitas tonight, and that scared me a little.

It would turn out, there were very good reasons for being scared.

Chapter Twenty-Five

At 4:30 p.m., right after Beck and Maeve left for the day, the Chief and Brad came to the back door of The Laughing Loaf.

With them were Sky Robbins and Dakota Li. Sky wore a t-shirt with an enormous hoodie and shorts, and his shiny, counterfeit Air Jordans. Dakota wore her knockoff silver boots with black jeans and a pink fake designer cashmere sweater.

In their interview with the Chief, Dakota confessed that she'd ordered from Eddie's operation five times; Sky had ordered three times. Both of them were familiar with how the ordering and pickup process worked. Both teens were familiar faces to Ezra and Laura.

So, with the Chief's assurances to their parents, Sky and Dakota had offered to participate in a kind of sting operation. They would order their goods on Aunt Dottie's site then pick them up at Eddie Sumner's house, as they'd done before. The Chief, Brad, and two Santa Cruz County Sheriff's deputies would be stationed outside, carefully monitoring the situation.

The five of us took our seats in the dining area of The Laughing Loaf. In the middle of the table, Brad set down a listening device he'd pieced together, using earbuds and an old phone scavenged from his other job. He'd spent an hour and a half watching YouTube videos on how to create and plant a DYI bug. He was clearly enjoying this part of his job.

"Dakota, carry this in your handbag," Brad said, with an air of authority. "If you keep it in the outer pocket, it'll have the best chance of picking up voices."

Brad took a swig from his can of energy drink. He was pulling a double shift, working the five hours of his Best Buy gig and then a full night of police duty. I handed him my phone, and he connected me to the listening device, so I could listen in, too.

"Now you both ordered through the website?" The Chief asked the teens.

Sky and Dakota both chimed in that they had.

Dakota looked excited about tonight's adventure, her cheeks pink. Sky looked pale and a little nauseous.

"I'll be close by, in the neighbor's driveway," I said. I'd wanted to be there for this. "I'll connect to the device via Bluetooth and listen in on your conversation. Brad and the Chief will listen from the truck."

"We'll hear whatever goes on while you're inside. Dakota, set your bag down when you pick up your order at the house. Leave it there," Brad instructed. "Pretend you're so excited about your new boots that you totally forgot about it. That'll let us listen to what they say after you leave."

"Got it. That's something I might really do anyway." Dakota laughed nervously.

The Chief looked the most skeptical of anyone. This wasn't the plan he'd come up with; he'd hoped to do a stakeout then a raid while the lights were on at the house. He sighed as he picked up the listening device components and looked them over. "I sure as hell hope this works, Brad."

Brad scratched his head and frowned. "I mean, it should work. Theoretically."

Both parents were shocked that their kids had ordered counterfeit goods. Sky's parents said they felt it would help him to cooperate with the police in the investigation, which surprised me.

"How are you feeling about what you're going to do?" I asked the two high schoolers.

Sky smirked and kicked his feet under the table. "Kinda nervous. These people are sketch. Not that I'm a fan of Eddie Sumner's, but if they killed him, I wanna see them go down. They also didn't think very much of us teens. They scared us so we wouldn't talk."

"Also, this stuff isn't made very well. This is my *old* handbag. It's five months old." Dakota opened up her "designer" bag and showed us the torn lining and cheap, frayed stitching. "It looked great for a few months and then it fell apart."

It was only 5:20 p.m., so I brought out sodas and some sliced-up toaster pastries for snacks. Brad and the teens started to dig in. When I saw the crestfallen look on the Chief's face, I realized I'd forgotten his dietary restrictions.

"Sorry, Chief."

He waved his hand dismissively. "Don't even worry about it, Gracie."

As we talked and waited, the knot in my stomach grew. Even if the bug did work and we were able to hear what Ezra and Laura said, we had no guarantee we'd get anything useful. I had a theory that they'd killed Eddie to cut him out of the business. But we had no proof.

"All right, guys." Brad stood up. He handed the earbuds to Dakota. She slipped them into the front pocket of her bag and zipped it up.

I sent a quick text to Nate.

Heading for Eddie's now.

"It's go time, peeps." Brad reached out to fist bump the two teens. "We're backing you up. You got this, guys."

Dakota and Sky went out to Dakota's car. I sat in Brad's truck cab, squished between him and the Chief. This would be an uncomfortable ride--but short.

The sun had just gone down, as we moved into our places.

The Chief had talked to Eddie Sumner's neighbors about what we were going to do, so as I stood along the side of the garage at the neighbor's house, I knew nobody was going to come out and demand to know what I was doing there.

To my relief, they'd also turned off their garage's motion-sensitive light.

I felt for my phone in my pocket. I put in my earbuds then watched from the shadows as Sky and Dakota went up to the door of Eddie Sumner's house.

Brad's bugging device was very sensitive. I even heard Sky's quiet whisper: *I think I'm going to throw up.*

I heard the knock, then the door opened.

"You're here for the shoe orders." I recognized Laura's voice, dull and flat. "Come in for a sec. I'll get them."

I heard what sounded like a box being opened. Then paper rustling.

"You had the Yeezy sneakers?"

"Yes, th-those are mine." Sky's voice sounded strangled.

"And yours are the Burberry plaid ankle boots, size 7."

"Yes, thanks. *Oh, my God!* They're totally cute." Dakota was playing her part well.

"Well, that's it. Enjoy your stuff." Laura sounded as enthusiastic as a bored tour guide. "Also, we won't be distributing at this location after today. We'll be mail order only. All the information will be on the website."

"Is there some reason you're changing?" Dakota pressed in, even though it sounded as if Laura was trying to shut the door on her. "It's just that this address is so convenient for me."

"We just are," Laura said in a monotone. "Deal with it."

I heard the door shut.

Dakota remembered to forget her handbag, because I started to hear the conversation going on in the house.

"I am *so* sick of teenagers, Ez." I heard Laura groan. "They're stupid. Why are we still doing this?"

"Because we are making money hand over fist, babe. What I'm earning at BlueSurf is nothing compared to the profit we've made selling this stuff. Now we're pulling in money from schools on the coast and over in Silicon Valley. These students are total suckers. Gotta have those names on their shoes and bags. Eddie had no idea how to take advantage of the market."

"But why did you have to kill him, Ezra?"

That got my attention—whipping me out of my end-of-the-day stupor like I'd just downed a shot of espresso.

I looked up to see Dakota and Sky slowly pull away from the curb and take off down the street. I sighed with relief. I'd been sweating profusely. I sunk back against the stucco wall, my damp shirt clinging to my back. They were safe.

I kept still, listening for the answer to Laura's question.

"I killed Eddie because he was no longer important to the operation. Sure, he used your import connections in China to set things up. But now word of mouth is pulling in the business with the teenagers. Eddie was no longer useful to me."

There was a pause, then Laura's voice, sounding nervous and shaky. "Ezra, honey. What do you mean, 'no longer useful to me'? Don't you mean, no longer useful to *us*?"

I recognized the click of a revolver being cocked.

I heard Laura scream.

In a sudden rush of noise and motion, I saw Brad approach the house, weapon drawn. Coming up behind him, reinforcements from the Santa Cruz County Sheriff's Department.

"Open up. River Grove Police," Brad called. "Ezra Dupont and Laura Freitas, you're surrounded."

In a few minutes, I found out the full story of what happened at Eddie Sumner's house.

After Sky and Dakota had left with their knockoff goods, Deputy Brad Castro, with help from the Sheriff's department, surrounded the house on Sunnyside. The Chief used his key to sneak into the back sliding door just as the county sheriff deputies arrived in a distracting blare of noise and lights.

With help from two deputies entering the front of the house, the Chief was able to pin down Ezra and Laura and make the arrest. After the two were taken away, Brad found a ring with the keys Laura had duplicated at Key Haus.

Brad played around with the small key for a while, trying it on any lock he could find in the house. We were all a little giddy after tonight's sting and arrest. I think, like me, Brad wondered if there was something else to be found on the premises. Maybe our success would continue.

"What about the playhouse in the backyard?" I asked, maybe because the scale model of the bigger house had always fascinated me. "Let's see if the key fits there."

Brad looked doubtful. "The Chief and I searched it. There's not much to it. We didn't find anything."

The mini version of Eddie's Craftsman house stood at the back of the yard, looking dilapidated. Brad pulled out his flashlight, and we ventured out into the dark, overgrown yard to see if the key opened anything in it. I turned on my phone's light and followed him inside.

After shooing a couple of rats from the playhouse, Brad shone his flashlight on a lock that was set into a panel of the wooden floor.

Brad turned the key in the lock, then pulled open a wooden panel, revealing a crawlspace four feet deep.

Brad sat back on his heels and started laughing, then I joined him. He took a photo of the space and sent it to the Chief. "No way, Gracie. Look at this."

It was stacked with shipping boxes. Inside the top box, we found a collection of athletic shoes, designer footwear, handbags, purses and backpacks.

All ready to be sold to local high schoolers via Miss Dottie's Yarn Emporium.

Chapter Twenty-Six

The next Monday, I was finally able to sit down with Maeve and Beck. We'd just closed and locked the front door of The Laughing Loaf.

The crazy events of the past two weeks had resolved Friday night at Eddie Sumner's house. I was exhausted but felt an incredible sense of relief.

After gathering up dishes and wiping tables down, we sat down around a table near the window. I set ube scones out on a plate, and Beck made each of us our favorite coffee drink.

Maeve picked up a scone and took a bite. She closed her eyes as she savored the flavor. "The flavor reminds me of donuts. But sort of nutty, too? I can't believe I haven't had this before."

"The color is beautiful," Beck said dreamily, as she held up a lilac-colored scone and stared at it.

I'd brought my folder with printouts of the proposed designs I'd received from contractors. This would be the first time I talked to my staff about future plans for The Laughing Loaf.

"I have an idea for expanding our service at The Laughing Loaf."

Both young women looked up in surprise as I continued. "As you probably know, there aren't a lot of options for lunch in downtown River Grove."

"Only RG's Pizza," Beck said with a groan. "With their fake cheese. Even when I was a kid, I didn't like it."

"Unless you want to drive down to Santa Cruz or into Boulder Creek, it's RG's and the pre-made sandwiches they sell at Corner Market. The Riverside's food service doesn't start till 3 p.m., so it's not really lunch. What I want to do is offer lunch at The Laughing Loaf. With fresh, made-to-order lunch options. Sandwiches, soup, wraps and salads. But this will change things—it'll be more crowded, and we'll need more staff. We'll need renovations to make our counter area bigger and more efficient. We'll need to rearrange our back room and work on adding more storage."

"And maybe more seating. Or reorganizing the dining area anyway," Beck said, looking around the room.

"We'll need more refrigerator space for luncheon meats and produce. It's a bit tight as it is, since we use it for cold rises for the bread," Maeve said.

I smiled. "See, you're already thinking about this. I want to hear these things. I have a couple of preliminary sketches from contractors for the front counter area. You want to see?"

"Of course!" Beck and Maeve leaned in to look at what I was pulling out of the folder.

"Oooh, the oval counter is gorgeous." Maeve looked at the design. "But would that make sense with our space? It looks a little confusing to people coming in the front door. Like, where would they go if they wanted lunch and weren't just coming in for coffee? Would it be just one line?"

"The long wooden counter would give us lots of room." Beck took a look at the long counter design. But if it's open underneath like that, do we lose all the storage we have under the counter now? Like the milk fridge?"

Soon we were engaged in a discussion of what we needed in order to serve customers lunch, both in the front area and in the back room.

A sense of warmth and gratitude flooded over me.

These two women working for me cared passionately about The Laughing Loaf. They were excited about the bakery growing and offering new things to customers. They knew the daily workings of the bakery and cared about the business. They wanted to make sure we did this right.

"Thank you, both. I want you to keep thinking about this. We'll meet next week and brainstorm again. I'd like to give feedback to the contractors in two weeks."

After they went back to work, prepping for the next day, I went back to my office. I picked up the square folk art painting Beck had given me two weeks ago—of me standing in front of The Laughing Loaf holding Biga. I'd tried to find a place to hang it at home, but it didn't look right in my living room or bedroom.

Now I took it out to the front area. There was a spot on the wall behind the counter, next to the shelf with The Laughing Loaf mugs. Here customers would see it, and my staff would see it as they worked behind the counter.

I installed a wall hook, then I hung the little painting up for everyone to see.

And it was perfect.

Chapter Twenty-Seven

My original plan was to have everyone involved in the Eddie Sumner case over for a picnic in our backyard.

And what could go wrong with that? The weather in River Grove had just turned warm and sunny. Spring was a few days away.

I'd lived here long enough to know good weather wasn't a sure thing just because it was March. At the last minute, rain was predicted for that Sunday. We could fit everyone I wanted to invite if we used the backyard, but not if we huddled in our small house.

Reggie McFerrin heard about the situation and offered to host the get-together at The Riverside.

Three weeks after the arrests of Ezra Dupont and Laura Freitas, twenty-five of us gathered on a Sunday afternoon in the large dining area of the Riverside Saloon.

The cozy inside celebration turned out to be much better than I imagined. A mesquite wood fire blazed in the river-rock fireplace next to the bar, filling the room with a woodsy smell. Manny, the musician-waiter, played classic jazz covers on keyboard up on the stage.

Reggie had laid out a brunch spread on a long table, so people could graze on appetizers and finger food. This setup freed people to mingle and talk informally with each other. At times like this, River Grove was at its best. All kinds of people, with different political views and income levels, chatting with each other like neighbors. I was surprised to see Carleen here, since she wasn't sure she'd feel comfortable at the celebration. She was at the food table, talking to the Schulz brothers from Key Haus.

The Chief, with Chloe and Mayor C beside him, chatted to the high schoolers. He had a right to feel proud of himself for his part in the arrest that night. He'd taken a chance by sneaking into Eddie's house from the back. He'd also asked help from the county sheriff, something he usually avoided because of his pride.

Mayor C took me aside as she moved on to the food table.

"I know the Chief was trying your patience, Gracie. Stubborn old men don't change easily. Thanks for your persistence." We both watched as Carleen tucked a handful of pulled pork sliders into her handbag.

I watched as other guests gave Sky and Dakota hugs and gushed with thanks for their part in the plan. I noticed Sky had ditched the Air Jordans, but Dakota still wore the silver boots.

Elana came up to me and whispered like the Wicked Witch, in The Wizard of Oz. "Those *boots*! I've *got* to have those boots."

You'"re not going to get them, my friend." I smirked at her. "Unless you're willing to pay for the real thing."

Elana looked back at the boots sadly. "They would go so nicely with my pink sequin jacket."

Kirk had been filling his plate at the table. He came over to us and gave me a hug. He looked thin and haggard, but then he was still working long hours to salvage a difficult product launch.

"Gracie, I'm glad this is all over. Thank you for scaring me into talking to the Chief."

I wanted to tell him he'd scared *me*—since that encounter with him in the woods definitely had a serial killer vibe. Instead, I smiled and put my arm around him. "I'm glad it's over, too."

My dad was talking and gesturing to Reggie, probably about chess moves. They had a look of intense focus—as if they were the only two people who existed in the world. I saw that concentration broken, when Mary Jo came in through the front door of the Riverside, wearing her red dress. My dad turned immediately toward her, his eyes lighting up. I'm sure that's when the chess talk stopped. Reggie got the message; he excused himself with a smile and went to the bar.

I knew exactly when Nate came in.

Mostly because he was always on my radar.

I'd been taking him dinners and spending more time with him lately, as he healed up from his pulled groin. The healing had gone more slowly for him than he would have liked. Today he entered without the granny walk. He leaned against the bar, gazing at me with a look I'd call smoldering. The corner of his mouth turned up and I blushed. I took a big gulp of my cabernet.

Me? I mouthed at him and pointed to myself. You want *me?*

I looked behind me, pretending to make sure he wasn't

looking at someone else. Then I pointed to myself again with a question on my face.

He nodded, and from the look of it, was having a hard time not laughing. He strode toward me, and I met him halfway. My heart was racing.

He reached out for my hand, and his touch sent a ripple of electricity through me.

"I hear Reggie has a balcony here," he said softly, near my ear. "Nice view of the river. And secluded."

"I can get us there," I said, urgency in my voice.

So we made our way to Reggie's secret back staircase.

Thank you

Thank you for reading
Proof of Death!

If you enjoyed this book, please consider leaving a review or rating on Amazon, Goodreads or the book review site of your choice.

I truly value the time you take to do this, and it makes my author heart happy.

Also by Victoria Kazarian

Drop Dead Bread - Laughing Loaf Bakery Mystery #1

Bread to Rights - Laughing Loaf Bakery Mystery #2

Trouble You Don't Knead - Laughing Loaf Bakery Mystery #3

Sourdough and Cyanide - Laughing Loaf Bakery Mystery #4

Stop, Drop and Rolls: A Laughing Loaf Bakery Short Mystery (prequel novella)

TRADITIONAL MYSTERY

writing as VL Kazarian

(Detectives Ruiz, Grasso and Flores):

Swift Horses Racing – Silicon Valley Murder Book 1

Across the Red Sky – Silicon Valley Murder Book 2

A Tree of Poison – Silicon Valley Murder Book 3

About Victoria Kazarian

Victoria Kazarian lives and writes in San Jose, California. After working for years as a Silicon Valley marketing professional, she taught high school English and actually owned a bread bakery of her own called The Laughing Loaf. When she's not writing, she enjoys baking artisan breads and forcing her children and dog to go on road trips to the Pacific Northwest.

See what she's up to at victoriakazarian.com

You can contact Victoria—or perhaps leave a message for Gracie Markley herself—at TheLaughingLoaf@gmail.com

Acknowledgments

Many thanks to my wonderful beta readers—Amanda Giles, Kerry Nozicka, Faye Friesen Myers, and Chris Anderson. As usual, you saw things I completely missed. Special thanks to Chris Anderson, who gets my timelines on track when my brain tells me that yes, everything in the book really can happen on the same day and time travel is possible. And to Pamela Milliken, for organizing and clarifying the Cherry Chocolate Sourdough recipe for me.

Thanks to my editor, Honest Magpie, for brainstorming and troubleshooting. And to proofreader extraordinaire Mary Ann Askins for finding my punctuation and consistency errors and those annoying duplicated or mysteriously missing words.

To my husband, Pete, thanks for your patience and the game playing breaks. Thanks to Debbie Cunningham for the incredible writer's breakfast!

And to the Sisters in Crime Coastal Cruisers chapter—I love that we accompany each other on our literary journeys. You've been great companions on mine.

Are you in a book club?

Interested in reading any of The Laughing Loaf Bakery Mysteries with your book club? I'd love to appear at your book club online - and possibly in person, if you're in the San Francisco Bay Area.

Contact me at thelaughingloaf@gmail.com

Laughing Loaf Bakery Recipes

Strawberry Toaster Pastries (homemade Pop Tarts)

Total time: 2-1/2 hours

If you grew up eating these out of a box, you'll be pleasantly surprised by the taste and texture of this homemade version. And they're easy to make.

NOTE: You can make these gluten free by simply switching in a gluten free cup-for-cup flour (such as King Arthur or Bob's Red Mill) that already includes xanthan gum. The GF tarts taste great, but without the gluten, they will be fragile. Making them smaller helps with the structural integrity.

Crust

2 cups all purpose flour

1 tbsp granulated sugar

1 tsp sea or kosher salt

16 tablespoons unsalted butter, chopped

2 large eggs - one for dough and one to seal the tarts when assembling

2 tbsps cold milk

Strawberry Toaster Pastries (homemade Pop Tarts)

Mix the egg and cold milk in a small bowl and set aside.

Thoroughly mix the flour, sugar and salt

<u>If you have a food processor</u>, put this mixture into it, adding the chopped butter. Now pulse till blended.

<u>If you don't have a food processor</u>, use a pastry blender (or two forks) to blend the chopped butter into the flour mixture. Keep blending until the mixture resembles pea-sized lumps.

After you've blended, fold the egg/milk mixture into the flour/butter mixture till blended and the dough holds together. Refrigerate dough for at least one hour.

Filling

1-1/2 cups trimmed, finely chopped strawberries

2 tablespoons granulated sugar

2 teaspoons cornstarch

1 teaspoon lemon juice

Combine these ingredients in a saucepan over medium heat. Stir and heat, for about five minutes, till the mixture thickens. Take off heat and cool.

After an hour, take dough out and roll it out on a floured surface, until it's a 9"x12" rectangle. Trim the edges to make the rectangle straight. Cut out eight 3x4 rectangles of dough. Lay out four on a baking sheet lined with parchment paper. Fill each with a heaping tablespoon of the filling, then brush the edges of each rectangle lightly with egg. Top each with a remaining rectangle, pressing down around the edges to seal each tart. Then brush the tops of the tarts lightly with egg and sprinkle with a little granulated sugar.

Bake for 20-24 minutes, or until the tops of the tarts are light golden brown.

Wait till they're cool - then enjoy.

Cherry Chocolate Sourdough Loaf

Total time: 2-1/2 days
Makes two loaves

Is it a dessert? Is it a bread? Why not both?

This is a time-intensive recipe, but so worth the effort. Be sure to read through the recipe a time or two before you start. There are a lot of steps to follow, but once you get the hang of it, you'll make this recipe often.

You will put together a special starter the night before you mix the bread, then you'll mix and rise the next day and let it rise in the fridge overnight. On the morning of day 3, you'll bake the bread.

The special starter for this recipe requires a small amount of ripe sourdough starter. You must have an active starter for this recipe. Be sure to feed your sourdough starter a day ahead, or even in the morning of day 1. If you don't have a starter, and want to try your hand at making one, there's plenty online sources and recipes. Or check out Gracie's recipe for Sourdough Starter in Laughing Loaf #4, *Sourdough and Cyanide.*

Starters can take up to a week or more to become mature starters, so be patient. It will be worth the wait.

The times suggested below work well with this recipe. While they are approximate, you can adjust according to your own schedule.

Ingredients

<u>Bread flour</u>
1/3 cup bread flour for special starter
4-3/4 cups bread flour for dough (for best results use flour with at least 12.7% protein content – such as King Arthur bread flour)

<u>Whole wheat flour</u>
1/3 cup Whole wheat for special starter
½ cup Whole wheat for dough

<u>Starter </u>- 1-1/2 tsp ripe sourdough starter (feed your starter the night before you start the recipe)
<u>Water</u> – Always use warm water – warm to the touch, but not so hot that you pull your hand away.
1/3 cup warm water for special starter
2 cups warm water for Dough
2 TBL + 1 tsp for later mixing

Dark chocolate chunks - 3/4 cup (can use chips)
Dried cherries - 1 cup and 1 TBL (sour or sweet work – whatever you prefer)
Unsweetened cocoa powder - 3-1/4 TBL
Canola Oil - Scant 2 TBL
Granulated sugar - 1 TBL and 1 tsp
Salt – 2-1/2 scant tsp fine sea or Kosher

Schedule

At 9 p.m. the night of Day 1
Mix your special starter:
1/3 cup all purpose flour
1/3 cup whole wheat flour
1/3 cup warm water
1-1/2 tsp "fed" sourdough starter
Mix the flours, water and starter together in a bowl. Cover and leave on the counter, or in a warm place overnight.

Next morning around 8 a.m. Day 2

You will "bloom" your cocoa powder by warming it in oil. This will bring out the rich chocolate flavor of the cocoa. Warm oil so it's hot but not crackling. Whisk the cocoa into the oil until the mixture thickens. Take off heat and let cool. Don't wash the pan yet, you'll need it!

Autolyse stage - around 8:30 a.m. Day 2

In large mixing bowl, add the 4-¾ cup bread flour, the ½ cup whole wheat flour, and 2 cups warm water. Mix till everything is folded together. If you need to, add an additional tsp or two of warm water. Cover the bowl and let it rest for 30 minutes. This is called the autolyse mix.

Mix dough - around 9 a.m. Day 2

Add the sugar, salt and all of the special overnight starter on top of the autolyse mix. Mix thoroughly, by pinching the dough into little balls, then squishing them together again.* When you've blended this, you'll add the bloomed cocoa. Pour that over the dough, then mix by turning and folding the dough over on itself.

Now pour the 2 TBL plus 1 tsp of water into the cocoa pan. Swirl it around to mix the water with the cocoa remains, then pour it over the dough. Keep folding the chocolate into the dough, until the dough starts to pull together into a ball. Now flatten the dough out in the bowl, then stretch and pull sides of the dough over the top of itself, turning the bowl to do it on each side.

Do not worry if your dough does not look uniformly "chocolate." As you fold and stretch the dough throughout the bulk rise, it will become blended so it is all a light chocolate brown.

Now transfer your dough to a container where it will have room to rise to at least twice its size.

Bulk Rise - 9:30 to 1:30 p.m. Day 2

Cover the container and place your container in a warm area - between 72 and 84 degrees.

This stage is when your dough will develop the most—and when you will do the most work.

Set a timer for 30 minutes, during which you will let your dough rest.

After thirty minutes, you will need to stretch and fold your dough. From this point on, you'll do stretch and folds every 30 minutes—up until the last 30 minutes (around 1:30 p.m.), when you'll let the dough rest again. You'll also add a little of the chocolate chunks and cherries at each fold.

Before you put your hands in to stretch and fold, get them wet with warm water. Now pull at the side of the dough, stretching it then folding it over on itself. If that's too hard to do, then grab the dough and let it hang down for just a few seconds. Gravity will be doing the stretching for you. You may have to do this for the first few 30-minute stretches. The farther you get into the bulk rise, the easier the dough will be to work with, and you'll be able to stretch and fold.

Throughout the stretch and folds, you'll be adding the

chocolate and cherries. Before you pull on the sides of the dough for your stretch, sprinkle about a quarter of a cup of the chocolate and cherries, then cover them with the dough as you fold it over. If you continue to add the chocolate and cherries this way, you'll be able to incorporate all of them by the end of the bulk rise.

Divide the dough - approximately 1:30 p.m. Day 2

Once your dough has doubled in size, it's ready to shape. If it takes longer, don't worry--that's normal. It could take an extra hour or more, don't rush it. But once it's ready, flour a flat surface and gently turn out your dough onto the floured surface. Using a bench knife/scraper, cut the dough in half. Shape each into a ball. Let the dough rest for 35 minutes, uncovered.

Shape boules 2:05 p.m. Day 2

After 35 minutes, dust the flour off the surface and shape each dough ball into a tight boule, by pressing down lightly and turning it. The friction on the surface will help the ball become tighter.

Then place each ball in a floured banneton or in a cloth-covered bowl.

Cover the baskets/bowls with clear plastic wrap or place them in a clean, unscented kitchen trash bag.

Cold proof in fridge - 2:15 p.m. to 9 a.m. next day Day 3

Set the wrapped baskets/bowls in an undisturbed place in your fridge until 9 a.m. the next morning.

Then preheat your oven to 450 degrees. Line your Dutch ovens with parchment (so chocolate doesn't melt all over your Dutch oven or pan) and set them in the oven as the oven comes to temperature.

Bake (finally!) - Day 3

When the oven's ready, carefully remove your boules from the fridge, flour the tops lightly, and score them with a razor or lame if you'd like. Then carefully set the boules into the heated pans and cover immediately.

Bake for 20 minutes, then uncover and cook for an additional 20-25 minutes, until the loaves are a medium-dark brown.

Let the boules cool on a rack for 2 hours before you slice into them.

If this technique is challenging, you can haul out your stand mixer, and using your dough hook, blend the ingredients in the mixer.

Deli Style Rye Bread

Total time: 3-1/2 hours
Makes one loaf

This is a hearty, nicely textured loaf of rye bread, with a slight tang from pickle juice. It's quick and easy to make and stands up to corned beef or pastrami just fine.

Ingredients
2 cups unbleached bread flour
1 cup dark rye flour
3 tablespoons potato flakes
2 tablespoons caraway seeds
1-1/2 tablespoons sugar
2-1/2 teaspoons yeast
1-1/2 teaspoons sea salt
1 cup warm water
1/4 cup canola oil
1/4 sour pickle juice

Mix bread flour, rye flour, potato flakes, caraway seeds, sugar, yeast and sea salt in large mixing bowl or preferably, in the bowl of a sturdy stand mixer with a dough hook. Mix thoroughly, then add canola oil, warm water and pickle juice.

Rest

Mix by hand or on the mixer's low speed till blended by shaggy. Then let it rest in a warm place for 30 minutes, covered.

Mix or Knead

Come back to it and mix for about 6 minutes on mixer's low speed.

Or if you're doing this by hand, knead it thoroughly for about 8-9 minutes, pressing in and forward on the dough, then folding it over and pressing in and forward again, so you're stretching the dough (and those gluten strands).

If you're kneading by hand, keep doing it until the dough is nice and smooth.

First rise

Form the dough into a ball, coat it lightly with canola oil, and cover with plastic wrap. Let it rise in a warm place until doubled—about 1 hour.

Second rise

After that, spray a loaf pan with cooking spray or oil it lightly. Form the dough into a log shape and let it rise in the pan in a warm place for 60-90 minutes

Bake

Preheat your oven to 375 degrees. When it comes to temperature, place the loaf pan on a middle rack in the oven.

The loaf should bake for about 30 minutes, until the top is golden brown.

After letting it cool for 45 minutes to an hour, slice into it. Enjoy!

Ube Scones

(River Grove High School Purple and Gold Scones)

Total time: About 3 hours
Makes 12-16 scones

Ube is a purple yam used in Filipino cooking. It has a smooth, creamy/nutty taste.

It also brings a lovely purple color to whatever you make with it. Handle the extract carefully, since it will also bring that same lovely color to hands and clothing. Make sure the cap of the extract bottle is on tightly after you use it. Speaking from personal experience here. 😋

First step: Grate 3/4 of a cup of **frozen** unsalted butter. Keep the grated butter in the freezer until it's time to use it.

Mix these wet ingredients together
1 large cold egg
1 cup cold heavy cream or whipping cream
1 1/2 tsp ube extract

1/2 tsp vanilla extract
1/2 cup golden raisins (optional)

Thoroughly mix the dry ingredients in a separate bowl, then slowly fold into the wet mixture.

Don't add the butter yet; you'll add it once you've mixed the wet and dry ingredients into dough.

Dry ingredients
3 cups all purpose flour
1/2 cup brown sugar
2 tsp baking powder
1 tsp baking soda
1/2 tsp kosher salt

When you're mixing these two, handle the dough gently and as little as possible, just enough so it's blended. If you touch it too much, scones will be tough when baked.

Once the dough is blended, roll it out on a floured surface till it's a rectangle about 3/4 inch thick. Sprinkle the grated butter evenly over the surface. Now fold the dough over on itself, and roll the dough out to another 3/4-inch thick rectangle. Now turn the rectangle 90 degrees, flip it over on itself and roll it out again. Then do this turning, flipping and rolling out sequence again (so you've done it three times).

Now you should have a rectangle 3/4 inch thick. Cut it in half, so you have two pieces of dough. Round each into a circle, then cut across each with a long, sharp knife, until each round has eight wedges.

Preheat oven to 350 degrees.

Place the pieces at least 1-1/2 inches away from each other on baking parchment or a greased surface. Bake for 20 minutes, then check to see if they're barely firm when you touch one.

Topping

1 cup white chocolate chips, melted (either microwave at 30 sec intervals, till almost melted, or melt at medium low heat in a double boiler. Don't over cook - when most is melted, take it away from heat and stir.

Drizzle this over the warm, baked scones. Top each with three raisins, so they stick on the chocolate. And if you don't want to use the raisins, don't! 😊

Follow me!

If you're on Facebook, follow me at **Victoria Kazarian - author** for additional recipes and content I'll be posting about *The Laughing Loaf Bakery Mysteries.*

Proof of Death Playlist

To enjoy singing along with the songs Gracie, Beck and Maeve sing as they bake, listen to the *Proof of Death* playlist on Spotify. Includes some Irish pop - suggested by new breadbaker Maeve Killoran herself!

Proof of Death playlist

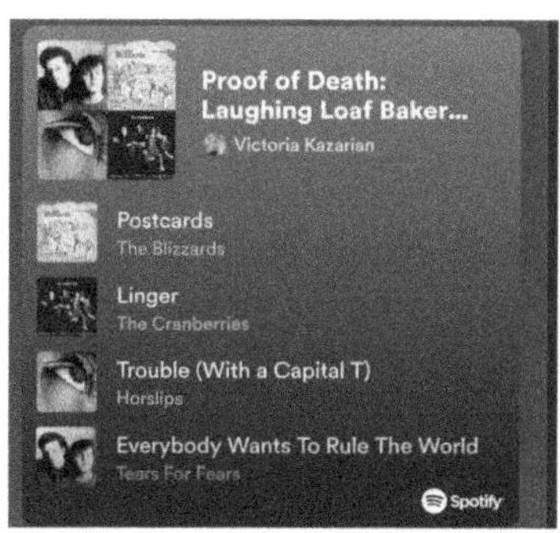